# The Runner

(Part One)

## *Nicky's Story*

by

# Hollie Bowrie

The Runner – Part 1 Nicky's Story

**Text Copyright© 2014 Hollie Bowrie**
**All Rights Reserved**

## **The Runner – Part One – Nicky's Story**

Already a successful TV presenter for a home shopping channel and with fan mail arriving for him daily from his adoring public, when Executive Producer, Lou offers him the dream job, it seems that thirty-one year old Nicky Ashton has it all. However, his private life couldn't be any less serene than that of his public one.

Rejected by his family for his marriage to Carrie failing when he finally admits to having been living in the proverbial 'closet', Nicky's had a tough and turbulent few years ... and it isn't getting any better with boyfriend Mike seeming to view Nicky as a possession, rather than a man to be loved and cherished. Furthermore, Mike certainly doesn't want Nicky to have any more success in his career than he already has; in fact what Mike wants is just the opposite; he's determined that Nicky will leave it all behind.

After three years' together, Nicky, growing ever more nervous of the previously hidden controlling persona of his boyfriend, has started to question just who the man is with whom he is sharing his life. Afraid to stay and even more afraid to leave, he's feeling trapped and unable to see a way out when he first sets eyes upon the young man on a London underground train; a young man whom Nicky suddenly seems to be seeing everywhere ...

The Runner – Part 1 Nicky's Story

# Contents

Author's Note ................................................................. 5

Dedication .................................................................... 6

Acknowledgements ....................................................... 7

Chapter One .................................................................. 8

Chapter Two ................................................................ 22

Chapter Three ............................................................. 36

Chapter Four ............................................................... 56

Chapter Five ................................................................ 74

Chapter Six .................................................................. 91

Chapter Seven ........................................................... 111

Chapter Eight ............................................................. 120

Chapter Nine .............................................................. 135

Chapter Ten ............................................................... 144

Chapter Eleven .......................................................... 157

Chapter Twelve .......................................................... 174

Chapter Thirteen ........................................................ 193

Chapter Fourteen ....................................................... 208

Chapter Fifteen .......................................................... 217

# The Runner – Part 1 Nicky's Story

## Author's Note

*The Runner – Part One – Nicky's Story* is a work of fiction. The characters and places are either the products of the author's imagination or used fictitiously and any resemblance to actual places, events or any persons living or dead is entirely coincidental.

The author asserts her rights to the work and no part of it may be copied, redistributed or reproduced in any form without the prior consent of the author.

Readers should be aware that *The Runner – Part One – Nicky's Story* has a theme of male homosexuality and whilst it does not contain any scenes of a sexually graphic nature, there are references to sex between men of consenting age within its pages. Therefore, this work is not intended for persons under the age of 18 and nor is it likely to appeal to those for whom the subject of homosexuality - in this instance love and sex between men – may be deemed as being offensive.

The image used in the design of the cover was downloaded from Depositphotos, copyright 'ColorValley'.

## Hollie Bowrie

*April 2014*

holliebowrie@mail.com

holliebowrie.weebly.com

## **Dedication**

For Phil

For unwittingly inspiring this story, for the generosity you gave in terms of your time and not least for the endless patience you afforded me in trying to assist to give it authenticity when 'poetic license' was simply unacceptable!

Thank you!

## Hollie Bowrie

*April 2014*

## Acknowledgements

My grateful thanks belong to author, Alp Mortal for granting his permission for me to use the immortal phrase of his character *Dane Danois* in his work, *All the World*.

My thanks go too to Philip Wood for his assistance in trying to set me straight 'behind the scenes' of a television studio as well as for the help he provided in his seemingly limitless knowledge of the train networks; both mainline and underground! Any errors within the text of such scenes are therefore mine to own.

Last but not least, additional thanks to Alp in his role as my very dear friend; for his usual love, support, energy and patience; all of which seem to have no bounds.

Hollie Bowrie

*April 2014*

The Runner – Part 1 Nicky's Story

## Chapter One

The first time I'd noticed him had been on a Monday evening in late January during the rush hour chaos of the city where he'd been sandwiched against the doors of the carriage on the Bakerloo line. He'd seemed completely unperturbed at being crushed and nor did he appear to be phased by the rocking and rolling motion of the train when he had nothing to hang onto to maintain his balance. With his rucksack tucked securely between his ankles, he had looked perfectly serene as he'd typed out a message on his phone; presumably ready to send the moment he could gain a signal. He'd boarded at Waterloo and had disembarked three stops later at Piccadilly Circus.

Why I'd noticed him I wasn't sure, other than the fact I had a habit of watching the doors, always trying to plan my own exit route through the rush hour crush once I'd reached my stop. There had been nothing remarkable about him to have caught my attention, dressed as he was in a pair of black jeans, a dark green hoody with some indistinguishable logo or slogan adorned across the chest, a black woollen hat on his head - which I'd found remarkably easy to imagine that his mother may have lovingly knitted for him -, a pair of once white trainers upon his feet which had seen better days and seemingly he'd been without a winter coat. With the rucksack to complete the ensemble, he had looked every inch the clichéd image of the student-on-a-budget. Guessing that he was an early twenty-something more or less completed my assumptions about the young man.

# The Runner – Part 1 Nicky's Story

I'd given him no further thought as I'd left the train at Oxford Circus to wander down to the book store on Oxford Street to collect a special order; the book having been the reason why I'd left work early and the cause of my deviation from my usual route of the Jubilee line from Waterloo where I'd change to the Circle line at Westminster in order to travel on to Victoria. I'd picked up my book, stopped at the coffee shop for a coffee-to-go and had returned to Oxford Circus station where I'd boarded the Victoria line train to travel to the station of the same name, enabling me to catch the mainline service to my home on the South East Coast and the miserable shit watching the clock whilst he waited for me.

Actually this last wasn't quite true. That he *was* a miserable shit was perfectly true but 'home' wasn't mine; it was his; a place in which he was King and I was ... in truth, I hadn't been sure of what I was to him. I did know that I'd no longer felt myself to be his prince as he'd once declared me to be and that I had been growing ever more wary of his swift mood swings. For more than a year my King had been ruling me with an iron rod; the equality we'd once shared long since gone; a sleeping memory without love's true kiss to awaken it.

Not a day had passed in recent months when I hadn't raised the question of why I stayed; a question for which I'd had no answer. Perhaps I'd felt that my debt of gratitude for the roof over my head had yet to be repaid whilst I'd continued to finance the family which I had left behind for 'misery guts'; perhaps too a part of me had still

# The Runner – Part 1 Nicky's Story

been lost inside my guilt and I'd considered my life now to be my penance for the choices which I had made. Whatever my reason for staying might have been, I'd supposed that in my loss of freedom, some might have considered that I'd got my just deserts for abandoning two beautiful children. Perhaps I had.

As the train had sped down the line, closing the distance between me and God alone knew what was waiting for me at home, I'd pulled my mobile phone out of my pocket to call him and report my reason for being late in answering my bail. I'd called his mobile number first, as his rules had demanded, only to be met with the standard network provider response advising me that the phone I had been calling was either switched off or out of range of the network service. I'd hung up and had dialled our home number. My call had been answered by yet another machine.

"Mike, it's me," I'd said as soon as I'd heard the 'beep' which had signalled that the machine was recording, "I'm sorry but I've missed my train so I'll be about an hour late. I had a call from the book store this morning to say that your book was in so I left work early to pick it up. I hadn't expected them to be so busy at this hour of the day. I'm now wishing that I'd gone at lunchtime. I'm so sorry ..." I'd closed my eyes as if doing so would somehow eclipse the final words; "I love you."

Grateful that fortune had granted me favour in providing me with a seat on a rush hour service, I'd gazed out of the window, nursing my phone in my hand and willing it to ring. I'd known that he'd rant and rave of course but as long as he'd picked up my

## The Runner – Part 1 Nicky's Story

message, I'd known too that it would act as a soothing balm to cool his fury. I'd watched as the stations where we wouldn't stop flew past and by the time the train had begun to slow beside the platform at Haywards Heath, my anxiety levels had reached a new high. Mike *always* returned my calls; if only to satisfy himself that the background noise fitted with where I'd told him I was. For the rest he had his own personal CCTV of sorts in our living room.

"Mike," I'd told the machine for a second time, "We're just coming into Haywards Heath. Please call me to let me know that you've got my messages ..."

I'd breathed a sigh of relief when my phone had vibrated in my hand a split second before it had begun to ring. My relief had been short lived when I'd seen the name of the caller; not Mike but Louise Felstead.

"Hi Lou."

"Hey sweetie!" my boss's cheery greeting had floated down the line to me, "I wonder if you could do me a huge favour?"

"Sure; if I can ..." I'd said agreeably, "What's up?"

"Jodie's just rung me; she's not going to be in for a few days," Lou had told me, "I can't say that I'm surprised; she looked bloody awful today."

"Yeah; I know. I saw her briefly at lunchtime. She thought she might be coming down with something."

# The Runner – Part 1 Nicky's Story

"Well, she has," Lou said, "Her doctor says it's 'flu. She's going to be off for the rest of this week and possibly next week too."

"Poor Jodie ..."

"Yeah; still ... the show must go on as they say. I wondered; would you be able to anchor; just until she returns?"

"Me?" I'd asked in surprise, "Shit, Lou; what do I know about jewellery?"

Lou had laughed, "It doesn't matter. Beth will run you through all you need to know each day and the autocue will do the rest. It'll be a breeze; trust me."

"What about my slot?"

"I'm not asking you to move for a couple of weeks, Nicky. I'm asking you to anchor for Jodie in addition to your own show," she'd said, "Naturally I don't expect you to do it for nothing. I'll make sure it racks you up a decent bonus in your pay packet next month."

"I won't deny the extra money would come in handy ..."

"You'd have to catch an earlier train ..."

"Yeah; I realise that but it's not a problem."

"Well, good. So; will you do it?"

I'd hesitated, "Mike isn't going to like it ... he *could* be a problem."

"I'm not asking Mike; why should you?" Her tone had become irritable at the mere mention of my boyfriend's name, "Jesus! You're not a child, Nicky!"

"I know ... but you know what he's like, Lou ..."

"It means an earlier train; that's all. What's it to him? He'll still be in bed when you leave!"

"Maybe ..."

"The additional exposure won't do your career any harm either, Nicky Ashton ..." she'd said cajolingly, "Not to mention the network. You pull in the viewers ... and you know it! Your loyal viewers will follow you across to Jodie's show and I'm damned sure hers will follow you over to yours; and once you've got them I'd be willing to bet that you'll keep a good percentage of them."

I'd laughed, "Thanks for massaging my ego, Lou. It was just what I needed!"

"Can I take that as a 'yes' then?"

I'd sighed, "Yeah; why not?"

"Brilliant! Thanks doll; you're a lifesaver. Need you in by seven ..."

"I'll be there ... though I'll be in breach of my bail conditions."

"What?"

"Never mind ... I'll see you at seven."

**oOo**

# The Runner – Part 1 Nicky's Story

"You're late!" Mike had barked; his arms folded across his chest as his cold and angry eyes had appraised me. Obviously he'd been listening for my key in the lock and had made a dash for the front door in order to berate me the moment I'd crossed the threshold.

"I'm sorry," I'd answered wearily, setting down my briefcase and stripping off my coat.

"Give that to me," Mike had growled, snatching the coat from my hands as I'd tried to hang it up on the coat hooks beside the front door, "It'll need to dry in the airing cupboard overnight ... it's soaked through. You'll catch your bloody death if you wear it like that tomorrow."

"I'm surprised you care ..." I'd said beneath my breath as I'd bent down to exchange my sodden shoes for carpet slippers, taking care not to allow either foot to leave the doormat before the shoes were removed and placed on the shoe rack.

"I heard that!" Mike had informed me, his back still turned against me as he'd stomped along the hall of the spacious apartment to the airing cupboard; a facility which was larger than an average hotel shower room.

"Well what do you expect?" I'd asked, sounding almost defiant as I'd removed his book from my briefcase, "All you ever seem to do is snap and snarl at me these days. I can't seem to do anything right ..."

"What do *you* expect?" Mike had fired back, hanging my coat on a hanger in the airing cupboard and slamming the door closed before turning around, his body filling the hall to bar my way as

## The Runner – Part 1 Nicky's Story

he'd glared at me accusingly, "Where the hell have you been until now?"

"The book store called to say that your book was in. I went to pick it up after work. Here ..." I'd thrust the paper bag out towards him.

He'd stared at it for a moment or two before he'd snatched it out of my hand without a word of thanks; not that I had expected any gratitude; that commodity was mine alone to give.

"Humph! You could have called to let me know ... I could have turned the dinner down. As it is, it's ruined!"

*Take a breath, Nicky ... or you'll really set him off.* "I did call; twice," I'd said calmly, as I'd dodged around him and into the lounge, "Try checking the answerphone messages occasionally ..."

I'd pressed the button on the answering machine which had still been flashing to show as yet unheard messages. Mike had stood in the doorway, scowling as he'd listened to my first voice recording; the third on the machine.

"Well I didn't hear the phone ring!" he'd snapped, pressing 'stop' on the machine to cut off my message to him before it had even ended.

"You can hardly blame me for that!"

"Why didn't you call my mobile?" he'd asked irritably, "I was in the kitchen; cooking your bloody dinner! You know very well I always have my mobile beside me ... *just in case you need me!*"

"I did call your mobile first ... *but it was switched off*," I'd retorted, my tone raising an

## The Runner – Part 1 Nicky's Story

octave. His expression had been enough for me to consciously find a lower, calmer register, "And you were cooking dinner for yourself as much as you were for me. If it was ready there was nothing to stop you from having yours ... so please; don't lay that one on me either."

He'd turned away, left the room and returned again moments later, frowning at the phone in his hand and visibly annoyed that it wasn't about to provide him with the testimony which would prove his point; that I was lying to him.

"Damn! There must be something wrong with the battery; it was fully charged this morning."

"I told you weeks ago that the battery was on its way out," I'd said calmly, "Why don't you upgrade?"

"I like this phone and you can't get them anymore ..."

"That's true," I'd said, "That handset is so old you could offer it to a museum."

"Oh, very funny Nicky ..."

"I wasn't trying to be funny," I'd told him, "I'm just sick of taking the wrap for everything in life that you don't like."

"What's that supposed to mean?" he'd snapped.

"It means that even I have my limits, Mike," I'd said, my heart pounding in my chest whilst I'd thrown my threatening words at him, all the while knowing that my threat was an empty one and wondering for the umpteenth time why I couldn't

# The Runner – Part 1 Nicky's Story

say the words. After all, a bedsit would be affordable, even with the mortgage and everything else I was still paying for ... and it wasn't essential that such a place should be near to Brighton's gay scene since I'd no longer shared in it. Being near a mainline station was all that mattered.

As the sparks of unspoken loathing had bounced between us, I had been able to feel the words telling him that I was leaving him worming their way towards the edge of my tongue. I'd almost choked in biting them back. I hadn't been able to do it, for the truth was, I might not have loved Mike any longer but living with him without love was a damned sight preferable to a solitary existence. Besides, the fire for a fight had already been dying in my belly. Not that the kindling had been lit often. Mike's temper had usually been sufficient to prevent me from striking the match. As I'd watched him watching me, I'd been able to see the embers of his fire still glowing brightly; all it would take was another log and it would ignite fully. One wrong word; one wrong look or small action and I'd regret my outburst, I'd known. There had been only one place I might be safe from his fury; if only for an hour or two.

"I'm going to bed," I'd finally managed.

"It's only half past eight!"

"I'm tired; it's been a long day and I've got to catch the five twenty tomorrow morning."

Mike had frowned, "Why?"

"Jodie went home as soon as she came off air today; her doctor says that she has 'flu."

# The Runner – Part 1 Nicky's Story

"What's that got to do with you?"

"Lou has asked me to fill her slot."

"So you'll be home early tomorrow?"

"No; it's not a swapping around of slots, Mike. Lou's asked me to do Jodie's slot as well as my own until she comes back ... and I've said that I'll do it."

Mike had shaken his head, "That's too much, Nicky ... you'll have to do it tomorrow now that you've said that you will but tomorrow tell Lou 'no'; she'll have to find someone else."

"I need the extra money ..."

"We don't need the money."

"You weren't listening, Mike," *as usual.* I'd thrown him a small smile, "I said; *I* need the money."

His eyes had narrowed, "Why? Are you planning on running out on me?"

*Not today; besides, I've spent my whole life running. I'm not sure I can do it again. Perhaps that's another reason why I stay.* "Don't be silly. I still have to think of the kids ... and Molly needs a new coat and a new pair of shoes. Carrie rang me at lunchtime."

He'd searched my face for a few minutes and the look in his eyes had seemed to suggest that my expression was as impassive as I'd hoped it would be.

"What about dinner?" he'd finally asked.

I'd raised my eyebrows, "I thought it was ruined?"

## The Runner – Part 1 Nicky's Story

"I can just about salvage it ..."

I'd shaken my head, "I'm not hungry."

"You have to eat something ..."

"I'm too tired; sorry."

After a moment or two, he'd nodded, although his expression had remained one of annoyance, "Alright; well ... I'm going to watch a bit of telly ..."

I'd smiled at him, "I wasn't suggesting you should come with me."

"No, I don't suppose you were," he'd said icily, his words weighted with meaning.

"You haven't eaten yet ..." I'd said lightly, "I don't expect you to starve on my account."

"Whatever!" he'd said, "Night ..."

"Night ..." I'd murmured; not that he would have heard. He'd already been flicking through the TV channels and complaining to the empty room about the pile of shite he had to choose from for his evening's viewing.

Funny really; there had been a time when I'd thrilled at the *Radio Times* being added to our shopping trolley, happy that I'd managed to bag myself a man who'd rather be at home with me than out on the town every night. Still; there's only so many times a person can take listening to the incessant complaints of another as to why they shouldn't pay for their TV licence any longer and it hadn't taken long before the novelty had worn off. I'd once joked how glad I was that I didn't work for the BBC but apparently my Channel was even worse and was amongst the many reasons why he'd

# The Runner – Part 1 Nicky's Story

cancelled his satellite subscription. Cheeky git; it was a free-to-receive channel! Not that pointing it out would have changed his opinion; the 'smarmy' presenters got 'right on his tits'. Perhaps I should have seen the writing on the wall then ...

Not that I'd feared Mike would throw me out; he had no more guts than I did when it came to ending our relationship. Besides, I'd been sure that he wasn't unhappy and why should he be when he was the piper piping the tunes? And in settling for second best, I'd supposed that we did at least still have something in common.

I'd felt him climbing into bed shortly after ten o'clock. Clearly he hadn't been in the mood for the evening news since there had been no-one to whom he could air his many opinions. I'd thought about feigning sleep when I'd felt his hand stroking my groin but my gratitude for the roof over my head and at least having *someone* waiting at home for me each day was greater than my desire for another row. Still; I would only have to show my gratitude for the few minutes it would take for him to reach his orgasm. Not that he could even achieve that without griping.

"God you're tight, Nicky ..."

*And you're hurting me; as you always do.* I couldn't remember the last time he had taken the time to prepare me properly, let alone allow me to actually take part. His 'wham, bam, thank you ma'am' attitude towards our sex life was sufficient to let him kid himself that we still had *something* resembling love between us. For my part, I'd gritted my teeth and had raised my legs higher; draping them over his shoulders in the hope of speeding up the process.

"Sorry ..."

It had taken less than five minutes of teeth grinding before Mike's grunts had signalled the end.

"I love you, Nicky," he'd said, placing the perfunctory kiss on my neck before he'd rolled out of bed, peeling the condom off en route to the bathroom bin.

I'd turned over onto my side, pulling the duvet up to my ears, not even caring that I hadn't had my own orgasm.

"I love you too, Mike," I'd dutifully murmured.

We'd both known that we were lying.

# The Runner – Part 1 Nicky's Story

## **Chapter Two**

The five twenty service, although having fewer carriages it had the distinct advantage of seat availability. My usual train, which departed from Hastings and being the last of what one could truly attribute to being a 'rush hour' service, was generally heaving by the time I boarded at Lewes. The five twenty was also quieter without the kids filling the carriage as they wended their way to their private school, disembarking at Haywards Heath and by which time I would already have selected the seat I was prepared to relinquish all good manners for once it became vacant. My morning commute was something of a ritual in this last and I had long ago learned who my rivals were for the precious seats if one didn't wish to stand all the way to London. Of course, they for their part knew me too and every morning it was simply a matter of pitting one's wits against another's as we danced around each other on the moving train in an attempt to be the nearest to the quarry we were each seeking.

I'd smiled ruefully to myself as I'd winced, easing myself carefully into my seat. I might have allowed my greatest rival, 'Mr Battered Old Briefcase', the pleasure of beating me to a seat this morning, for although I'd succeeded in slipping out of bed without disturbing Mike, the sound of the shower running had brought him to me and clearly he'd still been quietly seething that I'd 'ruined' dinner; that or he was still livid that I'd dared to refuse to spend the evening with him. Either way, when I'd boarded the train my arse had still been on fire from the none-too-gentle pounding he had given me beneath the powerful cascade of steaming

## The Runner – Part 1 Nicky's Story

water. There had been a time when I would have found his roughness beneath the shower to be erotic; would have considered such energy to be a raw, powerful beast of lust and need but none the less sensual for it. Of course, back in the day, he had been more thoughtful towards me too; preparing the way and opening me up thoroughly before entering me and once there, ensuring that pleasure wasn't a one-way street. Things had changed however; the new street signs had long ago been erected and the one-way street was fully operational; the direction being the one in which only Mike was travelling. These days, too scared of leaving the one-way street for one which might be leading to a dead end, I'd considered it to be my duty to 'endure' as I gave myself over to his will; the pay-off for my choice. And there it was; the key word; choice.

I'd shaken my head and had opened my briefcase; something *had* to change and my boyfriend of almost three years was the first change I'd known I needed to make; a matter which might have proved easier had I known how to muster the courage to do it.

**oOo**

"Hey Nicky," Louise Felstead, Executive Producer had smiled as she'd slipped into the seat opposite me, "You did a good job this morning."

"Thanks," I'd thrown her a small smile, as I'd torn open the pink paper packet of artificial sweetener to add to my black coffee.

### The Runner – Part 1 Nicky's Story

"Is that all you've got to say; 'thanks'?" Louise had raised her eyebrows.

"Sorry, Lou," I'd apologised, picking up the wooden stick which had served as a teaspoon in the canteen of the television broadcasting studios, "I'm a bit tired ..."

"Tired? You look cheesed off ..."

"Can't slip under *your* radar can I?" I'd mused ruefully.

She'd grinned at me, "You probably could but Judy in make-up's got a big mouth!"

"Ah!" My smile had broadened, "Yeah; I think she used a whole jar of concealer this morning just trying to hide the bags under my eyes."

"Hmmm; she said something similar to me ... about you I mean," Louise's eyes had flashed humorously, "So; what's up?"

I'd shaken my head, "Nothing ..."

"It didn't sound like 'nothing'," Louise had said firmly, "Judy told me that Mike had deviated from his usual Wednesday and Saturday routine."

"What?" My eyes had widened in horror, "Bitch! I told her that in the utmost confidence!"

"You told Judy in *'the utmost confidence'*?" Louise had snorted, "More fool you then! Jesus, Nicky; even you can't be that naïve! Judy's better than any gossip columnist ... and *you're* still worthy gossip material; even if you don't know it!"

"What; after three years; are you kidding?" I'd asked irritably.

# The Runner – Part 1 Nicky's Story

"No ..."

"Christ! It's not as if I'm the first ..."

"True," Louise had cut me off mid-sentence, "But you're the first around here to have left his wife and kids for another *man*. Newsflash Nicky; it still ... *fascinates* people; trying to work out if you're gay or bi ... I mean, you don't come across as being gay."

"You mean I don't fit the stereotypical profile of a gay man ..." I'd said disparagingly, "Well, sorry to disappoint you all. I'm gay ... one hundred per cent, *gay*. Pass it on ... I don't like being the subject of gossip. I feel terrible for what I did to Carrie ... and if I could take it all back, I would."

"What; even Molly and Finn ...?"

I'd shaken my head, "No," I'd said softly as I'd thought of my kids, "I could never regret them. Sometimes I think they're the only things keeping me sane. Still," I'd sighed, "It doesn't prevent me from feeling like a complete shit ... not where Carrie's concerned. She deserved better than some bastard who was so afraid of leaving the closet ..."

Louise's hand had stolen across the table to cover mine, "Carrie's forgiven you though, hasn't she?"

"Not really," I'd said, "And not that I blame her one bit that she can't. In her shoes, I'm sure I'd feel as she does ... but in terms of a public persona and for the sake of the kids ... well, let's just say that Carrie's civil; she makes it easier than I deserve ... but behind a closed door; she's bitter all right."

## The Runner – Part 1 Nicky's Story

"I think you're wrong, Nicky. Carrie doesn't seem in the least bit bitter; at least not to me. I think you're being a bit hard on yourself. I think it's *you* who can't forgive yourself."

"Do you?" I'd smiled weakly, "Then try actually having a *real* conversation with Carrie sometime; I'm sure she could soon divest you of your belief ... or any sympathy you might have for me. On the other hand; perhaps she really *is* happier with matters these days ... now that she can see the way things are working out with Mike ..."

"Ah! So that's it," Louise had nodded, "Mike; things are no better then?"

"Worse," I'd admitted.

"Then why don't you leave, sweetie?"

I'd shrugged, "I'm too scared to leave."

Louise had frowned, "Scared of what?"

"Being alone ..."

"You wouldn't be alone for long ..." Louise had smiled reassuringly, adding with a light chuckle, "It's true that your mailbag is full of proposals from women ... all of them *totally* indecent of course but then what do you expect from a bunch of frustrated housewives? ... but you do get a few letters in your mailbag from gay guys too ..."

"Are those letters all indecent too?" I'd asked; my tone as light as hers.

"Oh much worse ...!" she'd laughed, "Carnal ... I've read some of them *and* seen the photos they enclose of themselves and my God!" Louise had picked up a paper napkin, pretending to fan herself

## The Runner – Part 1 Nicky's Story

with it, "*Such* a pity they're all gay and you wouldn't *believe* some of the things they write ... mostly about the kind of things that they'd like to do with you ...!"

"Isn't there a law against that?" I'd asked.

"Not that I'm aware of," she'd answered dismissively, "You're thinking of stalking and none of them appear to be doing that ... yet. Christ! I'm telling you, Nicky. If only they weren't gay, I'd jump on their bones in a heartbeat! I'll get the mail room to pass some of them on if you like ..."

"You'll what?" I'd asked, throwing her a dirty look.

"Oh for God's sake; lighten up! I'm *teasing* you, Nicky," she'd rolled her eyes, "Although what would it hurt to take a peek and answer one or two personally ... or at the very least sign a photo personally; all it would take is a 'Dear Joe, with best wishes, love Nicky'!" she'd chortled, "Let the pen mark show through on the other side; they'll be beside themselves! I'm sure you'd put a smile on the face of one or two of your adoring fans whilst they're taking a shower!"

"Shut up ...!"

She'd laughed, "Bet you do it; over that actor you so love for one ..."

"Like I'd tell you if I did ..."

"At least the guys who write to you are gay," she'd laughed, "Imagine how your actor must feel ... since he's straight! He's got a girlfriend ..."

## The Runner – Part 1 Nicky's Story

I'd smiled in spite of myself, "Yeah; you all thought that about me once. I had Carrie ..."

Louise had shrugged and had returned my smile, "That's true. You know, Nicky, I *could* pull rank and take a proper peek at your mail if you wanted me to. Of the letters I *have* seen, one or two of them seemed to be really sweet guys nursing a genuine hope of meeting you ..."

"Not interested," I'd said, "I want something more than that ... something ... *real;* you know?"

"You want to be *in love* ..." she'd grinned, her hands cupped to hold her chin, her head tilted to one side as she'd batted her eyelids to mock me teasingly, "You big softy, Nicky Ashton!" She'd seen the retort on my lips and had reached across the table to pinch my lips closed with her thumb and forefinger, "I know what you were going to say ..."

"No, you don't ..." I'd mumbled through her fingers, making no attempt to pull them away.

"Yes I do; the second word was 'off' ... and there *is* a law against *that* in the workplace," she'd laughed, "Especially when you're directing such expletives at your boss!"

"There's nothing wrong with wanting to be in love and loved in return," I'd said as soon as she'd pulled her fingers away, "No wonder *you* can't get a man. You scare them all to bloody death!"

"Oh, I can *get* a man," she'd said, "I just don't particularly want to keep one ... in *any* sense of the word. Love 'em and leave 'em; it works for me. Perhaps that's what you should do; for a time at least. Do what I do; have the sex without the angst.

# The Runner – Part 1 Nicky's Story

You went straight from Carrie to Mike ... surely you don't want to go from Mike to another heavy relationship? Give yourself a break, Nicky; get out there and have a little of the fun you missed out on trying to conform to all that you thought your parents expected you to be ..."

"Didn't *think*, Louise," I'd reminded her morosely, "They did. They still refuse to speak to me ... and not because of Carrie I can assure you."

"I know and I'm so sorry that when you needed them the most they turned their backs on you. It's probably small recompense ... but *I'm* still here for you, Nicky; always will be."

"I know and I'm truly grateful."

"I wish you'd told me how unhappy you are ..."

I'd shrugged, "I thought ... *hoped*, things would get better. I'm in a rut and I don't know how to get out of it ..."

"Well you have to, Nicky ... and only *you* can get out of it."

"I know," I'd whispered, feeling the heat of the tears clouding my vision, "I'm just so afraid ... of being a failure; *again*. I *have* to make this relationship work; somehow."

"No you don't ..."

"I do," I'd asserted, "Besides ... I feel I owe him ..."

"Owe him *what*, Nicky?" Her eyes had narrowed and she'd stared at me in horror, "Surely you don't feel you *owe* him for giving you the courage to *come out*?"

"Perhaps; I don't know," I'd blubbed, the tears finally spilling, "He loved me; at least I *thought* he did ... and I loved *him*. I was head-over-heels *in love* with him Louise ... and he made it all sound so ... easy. With Mike at my side, I thought I could do *anything*; truly be myself for the first time in my life."

"And you *were* truly yourself for the first time ... and *you* did that, Nicky; Mike didn't do it for you. The courage came from within *you*, not him. Why can't you see that? It's still there, sweetheart; that courage you found. It's lost its way, perhaps ... but it's still there somewhere ..." she'd leaned across the table to press the flat of her hand against my heart, "In here ..."

"I don't think so ..."

"It *is* ... you just need to search for it," Louise had sighed, "Listen to me, sweetie; staying with Mike simply because you're afraid of being alone or because you seem to think that you somehow owe him something ... or even worse because you don't seem to believe yourself worthy of better ..." she'd shaken her head, "It's wrong, Nicky and you know it! I might not like Mike very much but you're not being fair to him and you're certainly not being fair to yourself."

"I know ... but what am I supposed to do; where would I go?"

"I have a spare room ..." she'd smiled, "More than one; you can take your pick ..."

I'd shook my head and thrown her a small smile; "Thanks ... but no. If I'm going to advance my career, I don't want any to be able to say it was because I got a leg-up through living with the boss."

She'd smiled, "At least none would be able to say it was because you'd been reclining on the director's couch ...!"

"Even so ..."

"Well, the offer's there, Nicky ... and I won't withdraw it; okay? If you need a bolt-hole, you have one."

"Thanks ..."

Louise had bitten her lip, "How about a bit of 'garden leave'; a couple of weeks ... to give you some time to think?"

"Oh good God, no; please don't do that to me!" I'd begged her, "A whole *weekend* with Mike is more than I can stand now ... never mind two whole weeks! Why do you think I took all the shifts between Christmas and New Year?"

"I'm sorry; I had no idea that things had got so bad ..."

"Well now you know ... thanks to Judy's big mouth!"

"I won't say this very often about Judy and her tittle-tattle but in this instance," Louise had smiled, "I'm glad that she told me. I'm only sorry that *you* couldn't tell me ... we've known each other a long time, Nicky. I thought we were close friends."

"I didn't want you to start watching me too closely ... on a professional level; wondering if I could still do my job properly ... with everything that's happening at home."

# The Runner – Part 1 Nicky's Story

"Nicky; I watch *everyone* closely," Louise chuckled, "It's my job! Believe me; I have no concerns about you."

"Honestly?"

"I promise," she'd sat back in her chair, raising the bottle of water in her hand to her lips, "Actually; I need to speak to you about something."

"Oh?"

She'd nodded, "Terry Jacks handed his notice in last night."

"Really; wow! I never thought Terry would go …"

"One of our rivals made him a tempting offer …" she'd smiled, "I'm only glad they didn't try to tempt you. I'd have been sorrier if they'd lured you away …"

"Give over …!" I'd said, feeling the warm heat filling my cheeks.

"No; I actually mean it," she'd said evenly, "And that's what I wanted to talk to you about; Terry's slot."

"What about it?"

"Its prime-time, Nicky," she'd smiled, "It would be a good move for you."

I'd sucked in a breath, "Are you serious?"

She'd raised her eyebrows, "I never say anything I don't mean; you know that."

"Good Lord …!"

"There is a catch …"

# The Runner – Part 1 Nicky's Story

I'd rolled my eyes and sighed, "I thought it was too good to be true! Well, go on then; I'm listening ..."

"As well as being a later finish, it would mean longer hours ..."

"Longer hours; why?"

"I wouldn't want you to give up your own slot ..." she'd said, "You're too good a presenter, Nicky. You have charisma; style and such charm ... and by God; you know how to sell. The lines went crazy this morning ..." she'd chuckled, "I think you've single-handedly redefined the words, 'credit crunch' ..."

"What do you mean?"

"I bet there'll be a few husbands doing their crunch when they get their credit card statements next month! They'll be above what they usually expect, I'll be bound."

"Thanks," I'd smiled, "I know sod all about jewellery but I hope some will think I've helped their wives to make a worthwhile investment!"

"Whatever; you did a better job than the autocue with your ad-libbing and I hate to say it; you did a better job than Jodie!"

"I doubt that," I'd pulled a face, "And as for the autocue; you know how I hate them ... although I'll be the first to admit, it *did* have its uses this morning since I hadn't a bloody clue of what I was talking about, regardless of anything you might think."

# The Runner – Part 1 Nicky's Story

"We had a sixty-five per cent increase on those trying to phone in to talk to the presenter on-air this morning," Louise had smiled, "I'm still waiting for the actual sales figures but I'm pretty confident that they will show a significant increase on those of yesterday and the same time last year."

"Perhaps the items on offer were more appealing ..."

"I don't think so," she'd said with a resolute shake of her head, "It's *you* Nicky. If Nicky Ashton enthuses about something then the audience gets carried along with him," she'd grinned, "Especially those who fantasise about getting inside your trousers! I'm sure some of them believe that you must have handled their products before they're shipped ..."

"And I'm sure you're exaggerating, Louise Felstead," I'd said lightly, "In the hope of giving me a swollen head and agreeing to increase my working hours on account of it!"

"I'm not ... but I *am* urging you to think about what I've said," Louise had said, suddenly looking serious, "Yours wouldn't be the first mainstream television career to have been launched from a shopping channel. In the greater scheme of things, we're small fry in the viewing figures but ... you've got better things ahead of you, Nicky. You're thirty-one ... anything could happen and for you it will. I can feel it; I know it! Prime-time exposure now won't do you any harm at all ..."

"Are you trying to get rid of me?" I'd asked, amused.

## The Runner – Part 1 Nicky's Story

"Of course; can't wait ..." she'd reached for my hand again, her tone earnest; almost pleading, "Will you think about it?"

I'd nodded, "I'll think about it; I promise."

"Good. I can afford you a week of thinking time; no more."

"That's really generous of you, Lou; I appreciate it."

"You're welcome."

I'd bitten my lip as my eyes had met hers, "Mike's not going to be thrilled. He told me last night to tell you to find someone else to fill in for Jodie ..."

"Did he?" she'd raised her eyebrows, "And is that what *you* want, Nicky? Do you want me to find someone else to fill in for Jodie?"

"No."

She'd nodded, had pushed back her chair and stood up, "Perhaps this would be the perfect opportunity for you to re-think your whole life; consider taking the plunge and going it alone." She'd pressed her hand on my shoulder, "I promise you, sweetie; it's not as scary as you think."

## Chapter Three

I'd raced towards the platform, anxiously pressing my way through the crowd, all the while able to hear the announcement of the imminent departure of my train and praying that it wouldn't leave without me. I would worry about sending up additional prayers for it not to be delayed en-route once I was safely aboard. *Oh dear God; if you're really up there and don't hate me ... please don't let me be late for dinner tonight.*

I'd reached the barriers, my season ticket in my hand as I'd joined the queues, cussing under my breath at having seemingly chosen the wrong queue to join whilst I'd watched the woman three places ahead of me having difficulty with the machine accepting her ticket. A porter had stood at the end of the bank of electronic turnstiles leaning on the closed gate reserved for wheelchairs, pushchairs and luggage trolleys casually observing the passenger, offering no assistance and apparently completely unmoved by her dilemma much less caring about the rest of us standing behind being delayed.

The porter's eyes had found mine and I'd seen the crease of his furrowed brow when he'd frowned at me, as if trying to remember something important. Suddenly his eyes had widened and he'd flashed me a perfect set of white teeth as he'd raised a finger and had pointed it at me.

"Hey! Aren't you that Nicky bloke ... the one on the telly; the shopping channel?"

## The Runner – Part 1 Nicky's Story

A couple of heads had turned in my direction. It hadn't been the first time I'd faced recognition of course but such moments were rare since as Lou had said; we were small fry in the world of broadcasting. I'd glanced up at the ceiling towards the disembodied voice being streamed through the speakers: *the train about to depart from platform fifteen is the seventeen fifty-seven service to Eastbourne; calling at Clapham Junction, East Croydon ..."*

Oh shit! I'd felt the panic rising, knowing that the doors would be closing almost immediately the announcement ended ... and I was so close; so tantalisingly close. I'd been able to see the train from where I'd stood, its rear end seeming almost to be mocking me. My only chance was the porter and the gate he was leaning over if I wasn't to be forced to board the eighteen-seventeen and arrive home to find I'd ruined dinner ... for the second night on the trot!

I'd left my place in the queue – what the hell did it matter now? I was going to miss the bloody train anyway - and had thrown the man my best smile as I'd approached him; my 'broadcasting' smile; the one which Lou swore could charm even the most reluctant credit card from any purse or wallet.

"Yes," I'd said agreeably, one eye on the man and the other on the rear of my train as I'd offered him my hand, "I'm Nicky Ashton."

"Thought so," he'd said, accepting the handshake, "Bought a ring off you only this morning."

# The Runner – Part 1 Nicky's Story

"Did you?" I'd kept my smile fixed in place, not liking to point out that he hadn't actually purchased said ring from me personally.

"Yeah; engagement ring for my bird ... not a real diamond of course but at that price, didn't expect it to be ... not that she'll know the difference," he'd frowned again as he'd sought my reassurance, "she *won't* know the difference, will she?"

"Only if she wants to insure it ..." I'd promised him.

"Oh, well that's alright then," his face had brightened in relief, "We don't bother with that kind of stuff ... premiums cost too much; you know? Bloody rip off merchants these insurance companies!"

"Perhaps ..." I'd said non-committedly, "I'm sorry ..." I'd nodded towards the train and then at the man's gate, conscious that the announcement had almost reached its conclusion.

He had seemed to understand my anxiety and had glanced behind him, "That your train?"

"Yes ... and if I miss it, I'm going to be skinned alive when I get home."

"No problem," he'd said easily, his actions unhurried as he'd generously unlocked the gate for me, "Come through ... so; how long will it *really* take for me to get the ring? Need it by Saturday ..."

"If you ordered it today then you should have it by Friday," I'd assured him as I'd slipped gratefully through his gate, "Thank you *so* much for this ..." I'd said, already beginning to run.

## The Runner – Part 1 Nicky's Story

"Hey; no problem," he'd called after me. "Oh, wait; Nicky ... Mr Ashton?"

I'd turned, continuing to walk backwards, noting the rush of the crowd streaming through the gate and towards the train; *my* train! Oh, now wouldn't *that* be just dandy? Every commuter boarding the damned thing before it left without *me*; and *they* would all be on time for dinner, thanks to my having 'sold' a bloody faux diamond ring to the unknown man!

"Yes?"

"Are you going to Eastbourne?"

"Lewes ..."

He'd nodded, "You need to be in the first four cars; train's splitting at East Croydon ..."

"What? This service doesn't usually divide ..."

He'd shrugged, "Don't ask me ... but that's where you need to be; cars one to four ..."

"Okay, thanks ..."

I'd turned and run, making a split-second decision to at least continue far enough along the platform to be able to enter carriage four ... it would be easier than trying to push my way through the narrow corridor and would afford me a better chance of gaining a seat once the inevitable exodus came when we reached Clapham Junction. I'd increased my pace when I'd heard the threatening sound of the guard's whistle and had observed him looking up and down the platform, ensuring that the doors were clear. He'd raised his flag, nodding confirmation of departure towards the engine driver

# The Runner – Part 1 Nicky's Story

leaning out of the window before blowing his whistle for the second time and hopping on board seconds before I too dived sideways, my movements resembling those of a speeding crab as I'd hurtled through the half-closed doors of my quarry; carriage four. Oh, thank God! I'd done it ... I'd made it. I'd sent up a silent prayer of thanks followed by my second plea: *I know this is greedy of me but ... please don't let us be delayed tonight!*

Finding a seat *now* would be impossible of course but I hadn't cared. I'd made it by the skin of my teeth aided by a fellow passenger who had gained purchase of my sleeve and pulled me firmly into the carriage, preventing my coat from becoming trapped in the doors; not that I'd supposed such a thing wouldn't have flagged up a warning in the driver's cab to alert him that a set of doors had malfunctioned, preventing him from moving off before he'd found the culprit delaying his train. I'd felt sure too that my coat would have caused me such an embarrassment, being of thick, heavy wool and screaming 'extortionately expensive' ... a Christmas present from Mike two years ago and a far cry from the carpet slippers of this last.

"Thanks," I'd muttered to the man who had given me his assistance.

"You're welcome," he'd smiled at me, "No-one wants to be left behind at this time of the day ... even if they're getting off at the next stop."

"No," I'd agreed, congenially entering into conversation with him, "And believe me; I truly didn't want to miss this service tonight since I managed to get myself into the most awful row for being late home yesterday ... and if I miss this

## The Runner – Part 1 Nicky's Story

service then I have few options open for me to try to redeem myself; even from Clapham Junction."

"Oh dear!" the man had laughed, his expression one of empathy, "Late for dinner were you?"

"Just a bit ..."

"The little lady was upset with you?" he'd sounded amused.

This was always the test whenever a stranger struck up a conversation with me and made reference to 'the little lady'. I'd swallowed and had returned his smile, able to hear my heart pounding in my ears, still able to feel the chains which had bound me to the lie I had lived for so long.

"My boyfriend complained that I'd ruined his efforts in the kitchen," I'd replied evenly.

"Oh." The man's grin had faded and he'd shuffled his feet uncomfortably before he'd pulled out the evening newspaper tucked beneath his arm, unfolded it and turned away from me to read it; or at least to pretend to read it.

I'd failed the test ... again.

Uncomfortable, embarrassed and feeling that my sexuality owed me an apology, my eyes had begun their customary search of the carriage, seeking out likely candidates for vacating their seats at Clapham Junction, simultaneously trying to judge which of my fellow travellers would be my rivals for such seats.

My eyes had made a double-take of him when they'd seen him leaning against the doors opposite

# The Runner – Part 1 Nicky's Story

those I had entered and it had taken me seconds to realise that he was indeed the same student-type I had observed on the Bakerloo line the previous evening. I'd felt myself stifling a smile to see him on his phone again, busily reading the screen before he'd grinned and tapped out a message at lightning speed. Yesterday, he'd had his back to me but now I'd been able to get a better look at him.

Standing at around five feet eight, he had a mop of unruly chestnut hair which looked in need of a good cut rather than being a style purposely grown long and to which blonde highlights had been added making it look as though straw had been caught in his hair. His chin and upper lip were covered not with a five o'clock shadow but more of a 'I really couldn't be arsed this morning' stubble. His eyes gave the viewer the impression of being sunk into dark, molten chocolate and when he smiled, it was easy to see that the top row of his teeth, although pure white suggesting him to perhaps be a non-smoker, were a little crooked. Somehow the teeth alone were enough to make me consider him to be cute. The jeans and trainers appeared to be the same as those he'd been wearing yesterday although the green hoody had been exchanged for a royal blue, crew neck sweatshirt which today he'd covered with a black fashion jacket; probably on account of the cooler temperature. Not that he'd fastened the zip! He'd abandoned the hat but had added a mutely coloured scarf of grey with thin veins of maroon stripes running through it to break up the single colour.

Moments after he'd typed out his message, his phone had rung and I'd found myself shamelessly

## The Runner – Part 1 Nicky's Story

straining my ears just to be able to hear the sound of his soft voice. Oh; cuter still! He had the smallest trace of a lisp and there was a feint accent too that I couldn't quite place; definitely not London; possibly Northern but where in the North I couldn't discern. I'd caught the name of the caller, Georgia and I'd heard a reference to Katie and another to James. It had sounded as though arrangements were in hand for the four to meet up on the proviso that James wasn't going to behave 'like a nob again'.

As the train had neared Clapham Junction and begun to slow down, the young man had abruptly ended his call and snatched up the rucksack secured between his ankles; the same spot in which it had been residing on the tube the day before. I'd been more than a little surprised at my disappointment in realising that he was about to leave the train and even more shocked to feel the sudden urge to disembark with him; just to see where he went. The smallest shiver had run through me when the train had suddenly lurched forwards as he'd reached the exit in front of me, sending him crashing into my chest. I'd caught his arm to steady him, feeling like a love-sick teenager when he'd thrown me a shy smile and muttered a courteous 'sorry' and 'thanks'. I'd barely heard my own responses of 'it's okay' and 'you're welcome' as my nostrils had been assaulted by the strong and delicious scent of his deodorant or cologne; perhaps both.

The doors had opened and he'd stepped out. I'd tried desperately to follow him with my eyes but he'd already vanished into the teaming crowd. I'd still been scanning the platform and the steps leading to the exit as the train had pulled out again but either I hadn't been able to see him or he'd already left the station. The strangest sensation of a lost opportunity had swept over me and for a second or two I had remained motionless feeling utterly but foolishly bereft. As my senses had returned, I'd realised that the young man wasn't the only thing I'd lost sight of. I'd lost the seat I had targeted to none other than 'Mr Battered Old Briefcase' himself who was grinning at me in his victory and probably equally as victorious because there were no other empty seats in the carriage.

**oOo**

"Is there something wrong with your beef casserole?" Mike had asked.

I'd looked across the table to see him frowning at me whilst he'd watched me pushing the food around my plate.

"What? No; of course not," I'd answered, "Why?"

"I've seen you eat five mouthfuls since I put it in front of you," he'd said irritably.

*What? Five ... fucking hell ...was he serious?*

"I'm sorry," I'd said, hastily shoving in another forkful, "I hadn't realised you were counting."

"Don't be so bloody facetious!" he'd snapped, "Jesus! What's the matter with you tonight? You've hardly said two words since you got in."

# The Runner – Part 1 Nicky's Story

'In', I'd noted; not 'home'. If ever I'd needed the confirmation that we were on the same page that small differentiation had surely been it.

I'd set my fork down on the plate and had picked up the red wine he knew I hated. Once upon a time he would have poured me white; regardless that it wasn't a perfect match for the dish we were eating. When did that change? I'd wondered. I didn't know; I only knew that I would never have dared to complain; would never have asked if I could have white instead of red. I hadn't asked then.

"I've got something on my mind," I'd told him, aware of his shoulders stiffening as his fork had paused halfway to his mouth.

"Oh?"

"Terry Jacks is leaving ..." I'd said cautiously.

"So?"

"It's going to open up a vacancy ..."

"Yes; I imagine that it will," he'd agreed evenly but already scowling at me, "What of it?"

"It's prime-time ..."

"Yes; I know what it is."

I'd returned my attention to the disgusting glass of red in my hand, sipping it slowly, hoping that it would supply me with much needed courage. I'd almost jumped out of my skin when I'd heard the clatter of his cutlery on his plate.

"I hope *you're* not thinking of applying, Nicky ..."

"No ..."

## The Runner – Part 1 Nicky's Story

"Well, good ..."

"Apparently there's no need for me to ..." I'd said, my tone as measured as his had been, although I'd doubted *his* heart had been pounding in his chest the way mine had.

"What?"

"Lou's already *offered* me his slot ..."

My words had been met with an interminably long, stony silence until unable to bear it any longer I had felt compelled to fill it.

"She asked me shortly after I came off-air this morning ... after Jodie's show."

"Did she indeed?" He'd picked up his wine, knocking back the remaining contents before refilling it from the bottle on the table, "And what did you say?"

"I said I would have to think about it."

He'd nodded, "You told her that you would have to discuss it with me ..."

"No, Mike; I told her that I would have to think about it," I'd replied, sounding a damned sight braver than I'd felt.

"But you're seeking my counsel ... right?"

"No; you asked me what was on my mind ... and I'm telling you. I've been offered Terry's slot ... and I'm thinking about it."

"You can't be serious?"

"Why ever not?" I'd asked in surprise, "It's prime-time; I'd be a fool not to at least think about it."

## The Runner – Part 1 Nicky's Story

"You'd be a damned sight more of a fool to accept it ..."

"Why?"

He'd raised his eyebrows, "Are you *nuts?*" He'd laughed, "Jesus, Nicky; even you can't be *that* stupid!"

I'd felt myself visibly bristle, "Why would my considering the offer to take a prime-time slot make me *stupid,* Mike?"

"I'd have thought that was obvious ..."

"Not to me ..."

He'd smiled at me indulgently, as though I'd been a small child incapable of understanding, "Because *my Angel,* the fancy, unnecessary baubles you flaunt before your adoring public, convincing them that they need these latest travesties of soft furnishing 'fashion' to accessorise their homes *isn't* prime time viewing; not even for a shopping channel," he'd said condescendingly, "When *men* get home from work, if they *want* to browse or shop from such places, then they want to at least be able to consider the purchase of things of interest to *them*; not the useless articles of interest only to the empty-headed bits of fluff they have to keep house for them!"

I'd stared at him in shock. Oh my God! Was I finally having my eyes forced open; was this the *real* Mike I was sharing the dinner table with; the apartment, the bedroom ... my *life?* Was that how he viewed *me?* The lowly, worthless, lesser 'other half' of our relationship; the fly in his ointment who had first managed to enrage him when I'd refused to

## The Runner – Part 1 Nicky's Story

surrender my career to please him in order that I could spend more time with him now that he'd sold off his successful, multi-million pound scaffolding business to sink into early retirement at the beginning of last year at the tender age of only fifty-three.

What the hell had happened to this man whom I would once have walked across hot coals for; shit! I *had* walked across burning fires for him. Fires from which my flesh was still burning in the loss of my parents, my siblings ... not to mention the fact that Carrie hated me and who the hell could know if my kids might not grow to share their mother's views; once they were old enough to understand. I'd fallen head-over-heels for this man who had spotted me sitting awkwardly at the bar on my first outing to Soho; the last I had taken without him at my side; wooing me, romancing me; making me feel loved and safe as little by little he had taken my hand and guided me out from the darkest corners of my closet. I'd been scared to death but Mike had given me wings and had taught me how to fly.

Funny really how quickly things had changed; all I'd felt this past year since his retirement, was unloved, undervalued, insecure and completely worthless. Slowly but surely the wings he had given me were being well and truly clipped. I'd felt sick as I'd continued to stare at him. Mike had managed to make me feel as I had probably made Carrie feel. The difference being that I had been a scared witless, closeted gay man trying to live within a world in which he didn't belong. Mike was, quite simply, a chauvinistic pig!

# The Runner – Part 1 Nicky's Story

I should have got up from the table then; packed my bags and left to catch the last train back to London and the blissful retreat of Louise's generous offer of her spare room. I hadn't. I'd sat there like a quivering lump of jelly; mutely seething at the ridicule of 'fluffy housewives' which I'd been sure had been directed at *me* whilst I'd continued to stare at him.

Mike had misunderstood and had nodded his head, no doubt satisfied that his work was done; sure that he'd wrong-footed me once more and in so doing had further fed my insecurity which in turn left me fearful to leave him, compelling me to stay. In that moment, I had realised that even his constant refrain of 'are you planning to leave me' and my endless denials were part of the control; a reverse psychology of sorts; as was the display of relief in his eyes each time I gave him my assurance that I did not intend to leave him. Everything he did, everything he said was part of the fabric of control he wove in order to keep me where he wanted me. The last thread to be snipped away was my career and suddenly I'd understood; could see the pattern of behaviour emerging. Jesus! I was hanging on by an invisible thread.

He had resumed his meal and had been speaking whilst I'd struggled to pay attention, "Do you see what I'm saying, Nicky? Move your show and the ratings will fall ... and who will take the wrap for that? Certainly not Louise *bloody* Felstead; *you* will! You will be out of the door faster than you can say 'Jack Robinson'. The wonderful Nicky Ashton will become a washed-up has-been," he'd smiled at me sorrowfully, "I don't mean to be harsh,

## The Runner – Part 1 Nicky's Story

sweetheart ... but you *have* to be realistic. Tell Lou, 'no'."

I'd nodded, "And if my refusal means I will lose my job because they want to move my show regardless of any objection I make ... because I refuse to be flexible; what then, Mike?"

He'd smiled, "Then you and I will get to spend more time together whilst you look for something else. I told you yesterday; we don't need the money."

"No, Mike; *you* don't need the money," I'd replied carefully, "I do. I still have the mortgage to pay ... Carrie and the kids to think of."

"I've told you more than once, Nicky; I will pay the mortgage *off* for you and you can sign the house over to Carrie if that's what you want to do ... despite the fact I would advise you against doing so but still; it would be wrong of me to try to influence you; such a decision would have to be yours ... and as for the kids; do you honestly think I would see them go without?"

"No but ..."

"I'll give you a monthly allowance, sweetheart ..."

"An *allowance* ...?" I'd raised my eyebrows, "As in 'pocket money' do you mean?"

"Don't be childish ..." he'd admonished, brandishing his fork at me, "That's not what I meant at all."

"Then what *did* you mean?"

"Nicky; you know how much I want us to spend more time together," he'd smiled, "If you

## The Runner – Part 1 Nicky's Story

weren't working we could do so much more; for one thing we would be able to take trips abroad as the mood takes us ..."

"So ... you're proposing to provide me with an *allowance* as ... what? Recompense for the loss of my salary?" I'd asked, "To enable us to spend more time together ..."

"Well, I wouldn't have put it *quite* like that, Angel but ..." he'd looked amused, "I suppose it's one way of looking at it, yes."

"Hmmm ..." I'd dabbed at my lips with my napkin before slamming it down on the table, "Well here's another way of looking at it, Mike. You're making it sound like you're my bloody *client* ... and I'm some bloody live-in trick rather than what we're supposed to be; *boyfriend and boyfriend!*"

"Don't be so bloody ridiculous ..."

"I'm not being ridiculous," I'd shaken my head, "I'm going to bed ..."

"Nicky; sit down!" he'd ordered me harshly, backtracking a little and his tone softening when he'd seen the expression on my face, "Sweetheart; I'm sorry; alright? I didn't mean everything the way it's obviously sounded to you. I love you; what's wrong with me wanting to spend all the time I can with you? Why do you think I sold the business? Why is it wrong for me to want to provide for you; support you where I can; when I have the means to do it?"

"Call it pride, Mike," I'd said making no effort to resume my seat at the table, "But I'm not a gold-digger and I never wanted to be a kept man. I didn't ask you to sell out ... so please; don't lay *that* one on my mat. I want to support myself. I like to work and I love my job. I'm not ready to sacrifice my career to suit *you!* Lou's offering me a real chance here ..."

"A *real* chance; are you serious?" He'd raised his eyebrows, "Do you honestly think that moving your show to Terry Jacks' prime-time slot is somehow going to advance your career; especially with the crap you sell?"

*Crap? Bastard! Don't bite, Nicky; don't bite!* "Stranger things have happened ..."

"In fairy-tales, sweetheart," he'd said smoothly, "perhaps."

"Adrian Fawkes is working for Channel 5 now ..."

Mike had snorted disparagingly, "Yes; as a *voice-over* to present the scheduled programming ... bit of a come-down isn't it? Presenter to *voice-over* ..." he'd smiled, "And if my memory serves me correctly, unlike you, *he* wasn't selling a pile of shite and being a smarmy git to suck in the mass of fluffy, empty-headed housewives, earning the right to waste extortionate amounts of money by spending nights on their backs with men who are too stupid to know any better."

I hadn't meant to take the bait but I hadn't been able to help it; despite the pain in my chest from my increased heart-rate.

"Why ... you nasty, spiteful ..." I'd sucked in a breath, "Just so that you know, *sweetheart* ... I've been offered Terry's *show* ... which should please you enormously since it means that I will be able to afford chauvinistic and selfish bastards like *you* the opportunity to be 'sucked in' by my 'smarmy git' presenting!"

His eyes had widened in shock and he'd paled, "What?"

I'd nodded, "Yes, that's right, Mike; *I'm taking over Terry's show ...*"

"I thought you were thinking about it?"

"You've just made my mind up for me ... I'm taking it!"

He'd stared at me furiously, "You can't; you won't be home before midnight ...!"

"So?"

"When will we ever be able to do anything together? It's bad enough now with you not getting in before half past seven every night ..."

"Ha! You never want to do anything *now* ... other than to sit in front of that fucking screen in the corner of the lounge and gripe about everything you watch! Where's the fucking appeal in *that* for me to *want* to be home any earlier?"

"Nicky ...!"

"And here's something else for you to chew on ... although I rather hope it chokes you; it's not just Terry's show I'll be taking. *I'll still be working mine!*" I'd seen his eyes widen further in horror and fury and I'd nodded, "Yes, *Angel;* you heard right. Those silly, fluffy, empty-headed housewives will *still* get to waste their lunchtime hours with this smarmy git whilst I sell them my *shite!*"

# The Runner – Part 1 Nicky's Story

"Nicholas!"

"I'm going to bed ... I'm catching the five twenty again tomorrow just in case you've forgotten."

"Nicky!" he'd pushed back his chair and had darted across the room to catch me by the wrist, gripping me so tightly it had hurt.

"Let go, Mike," I'd said calmly, "You're hurting me ... and I've had enough."

His eyes had narrowed and although he hadn't immediately released me, he'd loosened his grip, "Come and sit down; finish your dinner ... and let's talk about this; calmly."

"I'd thought I *was* talking to you calmly, Mike," I'd said, "But your idea of calm is telling me what to do and expecting me to bend to your will. I won't do it; not anymore." My eyes had swum with tears as they'd met his, "You're pushing me away ... and I have truly had enough. I can't do this anymore. Night after night, it's the same old, same old."

"What does that mean; you're 'not doing this anymore'?"

"What do you think it means, Mike?"

"Are you leaving me?"

I'd raised my eyebrows and had shaken my head, "As I said; same old, same old; same scenario, same phrases ... I'm going to sleep in the spare room tonight ..."

"Nicky ..."

"I'll be locking the door," I'd said calmly, "So don't even try; although ... you're so far up your own arse, Mike, God alone knows what you want with mine."

## Chapter Four

I'd smiled into the camera, listening to the assistant producer's voice through my earpiece whilst I'd simultaneously thanked Sarah from Chester for taking the time to call in to the programme.

*"Line four, Nicky,"* Rob had said into my ear, *"A guy called John; from Brighton."*

"I know Sarah's going to be thrilled with her charm bracelet ..." I'd given my best 'smarmy presenter, suck-'em-in' smile that Mike so detested, "... and if *you* want to be as happy as Sarah then you know what to do," I'd told the viewers, recapping on the item and phone numbers along with the payment options; all of which my monitor showed me were currently filling the television screens around the country whilst I had become the *voice-over* Mike had dissed last night.

The cameras had returned to me, "And don't forget; like Sarah you also have the assurance of our twenty-eight day, no quibble, full money back guarantee if you're unhappy for any reason; not that I think you will be." I'd paused briefly, "And now we can go to line four and say 'hello' to John in Brighton; good morning, John."

My greeting had been met with silence and I'd been quick to fill the void, "Hello John from Brighton. You're through to Nicky on Jodie's Jewellery Give-Away programme." Still I'd heard nothing other than the crackle of what had seemed to me to be an open telephone line rather than any gremlins connected to the gallery. I'd tried again,

## The Runner – Part 1 Nicky's Story

"Good morning ... John; are you still on the line?" I'd stared into the camera, the smile still on my lips, "Oh dear; have we lost John from Brighton?"

*"Whoever this guy is Nicky, the line's still open and I can tell he's still there,"* Rob's voice had chuckled through the earpiece, *"Perhaps he's shy or has had a sudden attack of stage fright! Try once more and then we'll cut ..."*

"Hello John; you're through to Nicky in the studio. Are you still there? No, we seem to have lost you; okay ... if you want to try calling back John, I'm sure my producer will try to put you through ..." Rob had already been feeding me the name and location of the next caller, "In the meantime we'll go to our next caller ..."

"Good morning, Nicky," I'd suddenly heard the voice being fed into the studio ... and I'd almost fainted. He'd sounded dreadful; as though he'd been crying ... a thing I had never known Mike to do in our almost three years together.

*"Nicky; are you okay ...?"* I'd heard Rob asking, *"You seem to look very pale all of a sudden ... Don; what's going on with the bloody lighting?"*

*"Nothing wrong with the lighting ..."* I'd heard the lighting director snap; sounding more than a little affronted that the blood draining from my face might somehow have been his fault.

*"Nicky ...?"* Rob had repeated.

"Good morning, John," I'd said, recovering myself and pressing my earpiece as though I had been adjusting it; the signal to the assistant

# The Runner – Part 1 Nicky's Story

producer that I had indeed been okay, "How are you today?"

"Not so good actually, Nicky …"

"Oh; I'm sorry to hear that …"

"No; I'm really not very good at all. You see, my boyfriend and I had the most terrible fight last night …"

"Oh …" *For fuck's sake, Mike; not now; not here …*

"I think he's going to leave me … and I need to tell him how much I love him and that I'm sorry; sorrier than he will ever know. I said some pretty awful things to him last night. He was offered a promotion at work you see … and I dissed him; made him feel worthless."

*"What the fuck …?"* I'd heard through the earpiece.

"I'm sorry …" I'd felt myself faltering on-air for the first time in my career. *For crying out loud, Rob; cut him off!*

"I've tried calling him several times this morning but he's refusing to answer his phone."

"I think you might have the wrong programme, John," I'd quipped lightly, "I think that perhaps you meant to call Steve and Annie's show … on the other channel …"

"I haven't got the wrong programme. I know he will … hear me through your show, so I rang to tell him how sorry I am … and to beg him to come home tonight; to give me a second chance … and to at least talk. I promise I will listen …"

# The Runner – Part 1 Nicky's Story

Mike had been talking at top speed; almost as though he had been on fast forward and far too fast for the bewildered assistant producer who had been slow to respond in cutting the call and had seemed to have gone into shock just as I had.

*"Nicky; I'm so sorry; I'm gonna cut this fruit loop ..."* Rob had finally said into my ear, even though little more than fifteen seconds of air time could have elapsed.

"I'm sorry; we seem to have lost John from Brighton," I'd smiled into the camera, "I'm sorry we've lost you, John and I really hope that you can sort things out with your boyfriend. If he is indeed watching then I'm sure he will know that you're upset and will give you a call just as soon as he can. I'm sure the viewers along with me wish you both well ..." I'd swallowed, hoping that Mike would understand the message I had been sending him.

Rob had been in my ear again; *"Go to a product recap, Nicky ..."*

I'd taken a breath, "I think this would be a good time to have a recap of all of the stunning items we've looked at this morning ..."

*"And cue camera three; cue Johanna and in three ..."* I'd heard the assistant producer's voice as welcome relief.

"... and the lovely Johanna can give us an update on stock availability ..."

*"...two, one ... camera three; Johanna ..."*

"Johanna?" I'd said in a cheerful tone as I'd passed the baton.

## The Runner – Part 1 Nicky's Story

"Thank you, Nicky. Well, to start with our first item; the charm bracelet bought by our earlier caller, Sarah of Chester ..."

*"... camera one ..."*

I'd seen the illuminated camera number and the orange light on top both go out simultaneously; proof that it was no longer running and a quick glance at my own monitor had confirmed for me that the live feed had switched smoothly to camera three in a smaller studio even before I'd heard Rob's voice. I'd finally been able to sit back in my chair whilst my heart had pounded in my chest as I'd tried to take some steadying breaths.

*"You're clear, Nicky,"* Rob had told me, *"I'm sorry about that mate; but good job ..."*

*"Nicky; it's Louise,"* I'd heard through the earpiece; clearly she had plugged in, *"I know that was Mike; I saw and heard most of it from my office. I came down as fast as I could. Are you okay?"* She'd obviously turned to one of the sound engineers, *"Have you cut his mic ...?"*

I'd almost laughed out loud; *Yeah; they've cut my Mike ...*

*"It's okay, Nicky; you're clear,"* Louise had told me, *"Are you alright?"*

"I'm fine; a bit shocked ..."

*"Who was that guy?"* Rob had asked; his question intended to be rhetorical.

*"Why didn't you cut?"* I'd heard Louise demanding of him, *"You gave him seventeen

*seconds of air time, Rob; what the hell were you thinking?"*

Although I had been upset with Rob for leaving me so long in the situation Mike had created, a part of me hadn't been able to help feeling sorry for him too. Lou had arrived in the gallery as a furious Executive Producer but in her self-proclaimed role of being my surrogate mother, the lines had blurred for her. She had been as mad as hell and mostly on my behalf; I knew that she wouldn't return to her office until I came off-air. I hadn't enjoyed being in my shoes but I certainly wouldn't have exchanged them for Rob's!

*"I couldn't believe what I was hearing!"* Rob had said defensively, *"He threw me off balance."*

*"Not good enough,"* Lou had said tartly, *"You know damned well that in this business we are not 'thrown off balance', Rob; not ever. I'll see you in my office at one o'clock ... and that's not an invitation to lunch!"* She'd returned her attention to me, *"Nicky, sweetie; you're off air in ten. Meet me in the lobby straight afterwards ... I've got to nip out to the bookshop in Piccadilly. You can keep me company. I'll treat you to a Starbucks ..."*

*Nice one, Michael,* I'd thought bitterly, *Rob's not the only one in for a lecture. Coffee and cake with Louise; always a bad sign.*

"I'll be there, Louise."

**oOo**

## The Runner – Part 1 Nicky's Story

"Tennyson?" I'd raised my eyebrows at the book in Louise's hands, "Since when did you read poetry?"

She'd laughed, employing her index finger to playfully poke me in the chest with almost every word she'd uttered, "I'm not a complete heathen I'll have you know, Mr Ashton."

"Really ... I had no idea," I'd smiled at her, "I wouldn't have had you down as the scholarly type."

"I'm not," she'd laughed as we'd strolled towards the cash desk, "My niece, Aimee is studying him ... the book is for her. She couldn't get it in her local town and I can post it to her quicker than her shop can buy it in."

We'd joined the queue and within a matter of minutes, Louise had paid for the book. We'd been about to descend the staircase back to ground level when I'd heard the lisp; a sound my brain had already added to its filing cabinet. Disbelieving of my own ears, I'd turned my head in the direction of the soft, quiet voice I'd shamelessly strained to hear on the train yesterday.

"Excuse me; I wonder if you would happen to have the Italian edition of the first *Harry Potter* book?" the young student-type had looked embarrassed as he'd mentioned the title of a kids book, "It's a present for my little brother," he'd hastened to add.

"Yes sir; I think we might have a copy on the shelf ... if you'd like to follow me, I'll show you."

## The Runner – Part 1 Nicky's Story

"Thank you," the young man had smiled, "I did have a look in the foreign language section but I couldn't seem to see it ..."

"It might not be in the right place," the assistant had said, "Very often customers pick books up and change their minds; if we're lucky they might return them to a shelf at least close to the correct section ... if not; well, you'd be surprised at some of the places such things turn up in; eventually!"

The young man had laughed, the sound of his voice already fading out as he and the assistant had strode away across the vast area of shop floor, "Yeah; I don't think I'd fancy being a stock-taker in this place ..."

I'd suddenly heard Louise laughing beside me and she'd swiped the wrapped book in her hand across my shoulder, "Put your tongue away, Nicky Ashton!"

"What?"

"It's almost cleaning the carpet!" She'd nodded in the direction where the two men had vanished from my view, "Is he gay?" To my utter chagrin I'd realised she'd been watching me, watching my student.

"Who?" I'd asked innocently.

"That customer; the one for whom the mere sound of his voice was enough to make your head swivel one hundred and eighty degrees. I'm surprised you didn't crick your neck, it spun so fast! Is he gay?"

"Not sure," I'd admitted, "I'm undecided."

# The Runner – Part 1 Nicky's Story

"You don't know him then?" she'd queried.

"No; but this is the third time I've seen him in less than forty-eight hours!"

"Really?" she'd raised her eyebrows, "Perhaps it's Fate ... or a sign."

"A sign?" I'd frowned, "Of what?"

"That it's time for you to find the courage to move on ..."

"Mike," I'd sighed, "I wondered how long it would take you."

"Oh come now, Nicky," she'd said lightly, "You knew I wouldn't be able to let the incident this morning pass without at least having to talk to you; it's my job regardless that I love you. I know it wasn't your fault and you handled it exceedingly well; I was proud of you ... but it was unprofessional ... and Mike needs to be told that such a thing can never happen again."

"I know," I'd said, "Believe me, Louise; no-one was more shocked than I was."

She'd slipped her arm through mine, "I know, sweetie ... and you were clearly upset."

"I've never heard him like that before, Louise," I'd bitten my lip, "It sounded like he'd been crying and ... well; it just isn't Mike; that's all. *I'm* the one who can turn the tap on; not Mike."

"Nicky; I'm not trying to pry; honestly I'm not and you don't have to tell me if you don't want to but ... you and Mike must have had one hell of a row last night."

"Yes," I'd nodded, "One of the worst for quite a while."

She'd pulled me to a stop, blocking the doorway of the store and forcing me to shunt her aside to make way for the customers clicking their tongues impatiently.

"You told him about my offer ..."

"Yes, I did."

"And it wasn't well received?"

"No."

"So what did he say?"

I'd thrown her a weak smile, "Nothing I would wish to repeat and nothing you would wish to hear. Let's just say that he doesn't rate our channel very much."

She'd nodded, "And he doesn't rate you either?"

"I thought you'd said yesterday that without Judy I would be able to slip under your radar?"

"I lied," she'd said simply, "Besides; I told you that I'd heard everything as it happened on-air this morning. Mike himself gave me the gist. Come on; *Starbucks* ... I'll buy you a comforting hot chocolate and a chocolate chip cookie ... and then you can tell your Auntie Louise all about it."

"Why couldn't you have been my mother?"

"Cheeky bastard! I'm not that bloody old!"

"I hate to be the one to tell you this ..."

## The Runner – Part 1 Nicky's Story

I'd watched her doing the sums in her head and she'd groaned, "All right; I'll have to give you that one ... although might I point out that I'd have barely been of age?"

"Eighteen *is* of age, Lou ..."

"Fuck off kid!"

"Hey! I thought that kind of language wasn't permitted in the workplace?"

"I don't know if you've noticed but we're not in the workplace," she'd smiled at me, "And this isn't the cake and coffee with Louise that you fear it is; I promise."

"It isn't?"

"No. I'm worried about you, Nicky."

"Yesterday you told me that you weren't worried ..."

"I'm worried about you on a *personal* level, sweetie," she'd sighed, "I as good as told you yesterday that I think you've reached 'crunch time' with Mike. He's pulling you down, Nicky ... you've lost your sparkle; at least off camera ... and it's all been since Mike took early retirement."

I'd nodded, "I know. I was thinking about that in bed last night ..." I'd thrown her a small smile, "I don't really think he knows how to fill his days now that he hasn't got the business to occupy his mind."

"Then perhaps he should begin another ... or take up a hobby," she'd said, "Suggest it to him ..."

"Christ no! It'd start another row ..."

## The Runner – Part 1 Nicky's Story

"Why?" she'd asked, as she'd passed through the door of the coffee shop whilst I'd held it open for her.

I'd smiled ruefully, "I think I was supposed to *be* the hobby; golfing with him, holidays in the sun; touring, cruises, seeing the world ... playing dominoes in the pub; you know?"

"Really?" she'd raised her eyebrows, supressing a grin, "Touring the world; what an utterly vile notion! Can *I* be his hobby?"

"You don't like dominoes ..."

"Details ..."

"You don't like him!"

"Neither do you it would seem!"

"I don't like him the way he is now ..."

Lou had shrugged, "Perhaps an extended holiday together is just what you both need ..."

"We might end up killing each other."

"And it might get things back on an even keel," she had suggested mildly, "And if it doesn't; well, at least you would know."

"Maybe ... except the 'extended holiday' Mike has in mind would take rather more than my annual leave quota; even if I were to take it all in one block."

"I've told you; I can arrange some garden leave ..."

"No," I'd said firmly, "And definitely not now; not after what happened today. Everyone soon learns of someone being on 'garden leave' and such

## The Runner – Part 1 Nicky's Story

leave is always on account of that someone being in *deep shit*. The last thing I need is to provide further material for Judy's gossip column."

"Fair enough; I get that … though garden leave is the easiest extended leave for me to arrange since I could do it today if you wanted it."

"I don't …"

"*How-ev-er*, there *is* another option," she'd said slowly, "if you wanted to take extended leave; to see if you and Mike can work things out … or even if you just wanted some space alone; to clear your head."

"What option …?"

"The company would allow you to take what they call a 'career break' …"

"What does that mean?"

"Well; you could take a whole three months off, Nicky; thirteen weeks in which you can be off on full pay with the guarantee of being reinstated in your current role under the same working conditions. In your case that would mean someone would temporarily fill in for you on your show; a thirteen week contract until you return to work."

"Really? I didn't know …"

She'd chuckled, "Very few do read the staff handbook from cover to cover … including you; obviously. It's all in there, sweetie."

I'd smiled, "It sounds interesting …"

"It's certainly something for you to think about," she'd said, "There's a second option to the career break too."

## The Runner – Part 1 Nicky's Story

"Go on ..."

"Well, you could take a full year off ..."

"I'll take it!"

She'd laughed, "Wait! This option has a slight sting in the tail."

"Oh!"

"If you take a year away you won't get paid; not a penny and although the company will guarantee you with a job when you return, it won't guarantee that it will be *your* job. You could be offered anything; including that of a lowly runner on a lowly runner's salary. You might even be offered a job with our sister company in Manchester and you wouldn't be able to refuse anything you might be offered. To do so would be tantamount to you terminating your contract of employment."

"Ouch!" I'd caught sight of the Barista looking at us expectantly and had nudged Louise, nodding my head towards the young woman behind the counter.

"What are you having?" Louise had asked me in response to the Barista's 'yes please?', "Hot chocolate?"

"No; I think I'll have a four shot tall latte[1] ..."

Lou had raised her eyebrows as had the Barista, "Are you kidding?" they'd asked me simultaneously.

"I'm tempted ..." I'd sighed, "... but yes; I guess I'm kidding."

69

# The Runner – Part 1 Nicky's Story

"Thank Christ for that," Lou had said, "For a moment there, I'd thought you were on some sort of suicide mission …"

"I could do with the caffeine hit …"

"It'd hit something …" Louise had said drily, turning back to the Barista, "He doesn't even *take* milk; give him a *tall* black coffee … with *one* extra shot … and an Americano; standard."

"Thanks …" I'd grinned at her.

"*Four shot tall latte!* Pah!" she'd said disparagingly, "The very idea! What the *hell* made you think of *that*?"

"I'd like to take the credit but it's the opening gambit of the book I'm currently reading …"

"What?" She'd frowned at me.

"It's the favourite tipple of the main protagonist … I've thought about trying it on Mike a few times of late; just to see what would happen …"

"It would give him fucking tachycardia I should think …"

"It's a nice dream …"

"Dreaming of serving Mike coffee high in caffeine?" she'd asked as I'd picked up our tray and followed her to a vacant table.

"Dreaming of Mike having a heart attack …"

"Nicky! That's a terrible thing to say …" she'd said, peeling her coat off and hanging it over the back of her chair before sitting down.

I'd sighed, "I know … but sometimes; well, I suppose there are just times when such awful thoughts seem to be the ideal; of providing me with an easy exit; you know?"

"I thought you were afraid of being alone?"

"I am ... but if I don't have to make the choice ..."

"Perhaps Mike will end it?"

"No he won't, just as he knows I won't! You heard him this morning ... although don't believe the bit about him loving me. Mike's just as afraid of being alone as I am ... and I'm handy to have around; for the most part. He needs someone to air his opinions too; to gripe to about whatever displeases or irritates him and for everything that he feels is wrong in his life he needs someone to blame ... and more than anything he needs someone he knows is too afraid to argue with him; all of which adds up to ... me. If he loves me then he does so for about five minutes twice a week ... on Wednesday's and Saturday's."

"Oooh; that's not good ..."

"Not for me it isn't ..."

Lou had sighed whilst she'd gazed at me through sad eyes, "Do you think this might just be a 'blip' in your relationship? Might you both just be having a hard time adjusting to the changes?"

"No; it's gone way beyond that."

"Then *leave him*, Nicky ..."

"I can't."

"Why ever not?"

"Oh God; I don't know!"

## The Runner – Part 1 Nicky's Story

"Nicky; do you still love him?" Louise had asked gently, "Is that what's holding you back? He's pissing you off but somewhere deep down, you still love him?"

I'd shaken my head, "No; that's not it at all. I *care* about him but ..."

"It's not the same thing ..."

"No."

"In that case it seems to me that you have two choices, Nicky," she'd said leaning back in her chair and folding her arms across her chest, "The first is that you stay and accept that you're going to be thoroughly miserable; possibly for the rest of your life ... and the second is that you find some balls, leave and start again."

I'd smiled wanly, "Isn't there a third choice; a better one?"

She'd shaken her head, "Sorry, no."

"Thanks; so I'm right back where I started!"

"Do you really want to know what I think, Nicky?"

I'd nodded, "Just be gentle with me ..."

She'd smiled but there was little humour to be seen in it, "I think Mike has become your new closet."

"What?"

She'd shrugged, "It's just my perspective, sweetheart. You venture out onto the gay scene for the first time, meet Mike the same night and before long you've left one closet for another." She'd

# The Runner – Part 1 Nicky's Story

smiled, "I think you need to come out of the closet again, Nicky ... and this time be sure that you're doing it for yourself."

[1] *Four shot tall latte – taken, with kind permission, from 'All the World' – Alp Mortal*

## Chapter Five

He'd been about fifty yards ahead of me as we'd entered the station at Waterloo. I hadn't really noticed his outfit when I'd seen him in the book store in Piccadilly as my attention had been focused entirely upon his face and voice but despite the people hurrying to make their way underground even at three in the afternoon, I'd known it was my student from the manner of his walk alone; something else my unconscious mind had stored on my behalf and a fact which had startled me more than a little.

I'd expected him to head towards the Bakerloo line since it was on this part of London's underground network where I'd first clapped eyes on him forty-eight hours previously. He hadn't; instead he'd turned his steps towards the Northern line, calmly checking his watch whilst people pushed their way past, jostling him and rocking him on his feet. If it had annoyed him, he'd given no outward sign of it having done so, his demeanour one of perfect serenity as his feet had continued to steer him towards the platform where he'd glanced up at the information boards announcing that the next train was due in two minutes.

My eyes had followed his, causing me a moment of bewildered confusion to see that the inbound train was destined for Edgware rather than Harrow and Wealdstone and I'd been startled for the second time in less than a minute to realise that I'd followed him; almost as though some invisible thread had momentarily been joining us together and forcing me to follow where he'd led. The thread

# The Runner – Part 1 Nicky's Story

had snapped and in so doing had restored me to my senses. I'd been about to retrace my steps towards the Jubilee line when his eyes had suddenly met mine. Although he hadn't smiled, he'd given me the smallest nod of recognition. My heart had joyfully welcomed the missed beat as I'd understood that he'd remembered me from the nanoseconds of physical contact between us when the train had lurched forwards at Clapham Junction on the previous evening.

In the time it had taken for the passenger information board to update the ticker announcing that the train was 'due' and confident that like me he was heading towards Victoria to pick up a train which would take him on to Clapham Junction, I'd reassessed my journey; partly from wanting to disembark with him and follow him to Victoria where if Lady Luck was on my side, he would board my train again. An even better thought was that should the said Lady be feeling particularly generous, perhaps on this earlier service I would even be able to find a seat; one near to him and from where I could surreptitiously observe him until he alighted at Clapham Junction.

My second reason for not having left the platform had been borne from an irrational fear that with my student having just acknowledged me, if by some miracle he should have happened to have noticed *me* as I had him on the two occasions other than the one in which we had collided and if I were to turn tail now, he might begin to suspect that he had caught me stalking him; and after all, I could alight just as easily at Embankment as Westminster to change lines to Victoria.

# The Runner – Part 1 Nicky's Story

*You are stalking him, Nicky!* My inner self had chastised me. *No, I'm not,* I'd retorted defensively, *I just want to strike up a conversation with him … and before you ask; I don't know why!* It was true; I didn't … but there was something about the young student which was drawing me to him like a moth to a flame; almost as though he had woken something in me that had long since fallen asleep. Whatever it was that was sleeping, all it had wanted was the soft and tender kiss of a prince …

I'd heard the soft laughter of my inner self; *whatever ridiculous notions you're forming Nicky Ashton; need I remind you that you're attached? Mike's waiting for you at home!* My heart had fallen into my stomach; *Yeah; thanks for that; I know!*

Standing some distance apart from him, when the train had drawn into the platform, I'd felt a small pang of disappointment to see that the sets of doors had been lining up to both him and me with unerring perfection as the train had slowed and stopped; giving me no reason to turn my steps in his direction to enter the carriage through the same set of doors as those through which he was boarding. It didn't matter; as luck would have it, both sets of doors had led to the interior of the same carriage.

I'd watched him move towards an empty seat, noting to my delight that the seat beside him was also empty. Although it was only one stop from Waterloo to Embankment, I'd rushed towards it, tripping over somebody's shopping bags en route, murmuring a quick apology, despite the fact that I'd cussed inwardly at the inconsideration of the shopper not to have ensured my safe passage

## The Runner – Part 1 Nicky's Story

through the carriage. I'd cussed again when I'd seen the huge bottom of the large woman wriggling her arse into the seat next to my student, forcing him to shift over very slightly in his own seat to free his hip and thigh from the woman's plentiful flesh. I'd felt that the woman dropping her ticket onto the dirty floor had been deserved and appropriate penance for having stolen the seat which was meant to be mine. My glee in watching her struggle to lean over her ample frame in a bid to retrieve it had faded almost instantly to those of shame and guilt for such ungenerous thoughts which were far removed from those of my true nature. *You've been with Mike for far too long, Nicky Ashton,* I'd admonished myself ruefully.

I'd reacted too late to make amends for the spiteful thoughts to which the woman had been blissfully unaware, for as I'd bent to retrieve the ticket, my student had already picked it up and I'd straightened my back to watch him return it to his neighbour with nothing more than a smile. As the woman had offered him her thanks, he'd given her another small smile and a nod of his head before turning his attention to pulling his iPod out of the pocket of the same jacket he'd been wearing yesterday and pushing a set of headphones into his ears. The small action had been compensation to me of sorts for my lost seat beside him, since being wired into the small device would have robbed me of any opportunity of striking up a conversation with him; though what I'd imagined I might have said, I'd had no idea. My public persona in front of the cameras was a far cry from the reticence I usually preferred to keep company with in private.

## The Runner – Part 1 Nicky's Story

As the train had pulled into Embankment, still fearful that he would be 'onto me' had he seen me following him from the train, I'd made my way towards the doors before my student had left his seat, not minding in the least since I'd been confident that like me, he'd been making his way home early and I'd been just as certain that I wouldn't have too long to wait before I could 'accidentally on purpose' meet him again on the Southbound mainline train. I'd almost reached the exit point from the platform when the train had moved off and I had turned my head almost reflexively as it had begun to pass me.

My heart had plummeted downwards to share space in my shoes with my feet as I'd seen my student still plugged into his iPod ... and still on the train.

**oOo**

"Nicky?"

I'd barely set my briefcase down beneath the bank of coat hooks as I was required to do, when Mike had hurried into the hall to meet me. He'd been expecting me of course as I'd called him from the train within minutes of it leaving Victoria to tell him that I'd asked Lou to take me off-air in order that I could leave early. Far from looking contrite, the expression on his face had been sufficient for me to know that the quick, rather flippant *'sorry about earlier'* I'd received over the phone was all I could expect. In that moment, he'd reminded me of my seven year old son, Finn caught in some petty

## The Runner – Part 1 Nicky's Story

misdemeanour and sorry not for his actions but rather at the ticking off he felt to be unjustified.

"Hi," I'd said quietly, obediently turning around when he'd circled his index finger and stepped up behind me to peel my coat away from my shoulders; hanging it up for me in the airing cupboard as he'd done yesterday whilst I'd exchanged my shoes for the carpet slippers he'd bought me for Christmas.

"I know you're upset with me, Angel," he'd called out from inside the airing cupboard, "And I don't blame you one bit; it was a stupid thing for me to have done. However, I don't think we should dwell on it ..." he'd reappeared to throw me a jolly smile, "Best we forget it ever happened and move on."

"I could have lost my job, Mike ..."

"For something *I* did?" he'd shaken his head, "I don't think so, sweetheart and even if you had, no tribunal would have found in their favour. You can hardly be held responsible for *my* actions."

"Perhaps you should tell that to Rob Watts," I'd said drily, still watching him from my place on the doormat, "On account of *your* actions, he's now the proud owner of a recorded verbal warning on his personnel file; a record that was previously unblemished."

He'd raised his eyebrows, "And Rob Watts is ...?"

"Assistant Producer ..." I'd said, "He was so stunned, he gave you a little too much air time ..."

"Ah! Well in his case, I'd say the punishment was justified; it was his job ..."

## The Runner – Part 1 Nicky's Story

I'd rolled my eyes in frustration and despair. My colleague's disciplinary wasn't an argument I'd wanted to get into with Mike; regardless that he'd made me feel responsible for Rob's now tarnished file. It wouldn't have mattered what I'd said; Mike would somehow have managed to tie me up in knots to place me firmly in the wrong and I was still feeling drained from the stand I had taken against him on the previous evening, never mind the shock he'd given me this morning.

"What the hell were you thinking, Michael?" I'd said instead.

"I was drunk …"

*Drunk? Of course! I should have known; should have realised.* Excess drink and Mike was a relationship which usually ended in tears of self-pity. It hadn't been quite true when I'd told Lou that I'd never known him to get into such a state … of course I had. I just hadn't considered that drink might have been responsible for this morning's little 'episode'. Perhaps Louise had been right; perhaps a part of me did still love him and in so doing I had wanted to believe that despite my embarrassment this morning, it had been the proof I'd needed that he *did* love me; that when I returned home he would plead with me to stay; swear to me that things would change; get better … and that he would actually be sincere and mean it. I should have known that drink had been talking a good talk on his behalf.

"You were *drunk*; by *quarter to eleven* in the morning?"

# The Runner – Part 1 Nicky's Story

"I was upset! You refused to sleep in our bed last night ..." he'd smiled, "... and let's face it; you *do* have a tendency to over-react, Nicky and I know that you talk to Lou. She's never liked me and it occurred to me that she might not waste the chance to put the boot in; convince you to leave me ... and you *did* go off to work without a word this morning ..."

"I left at *ten to five,* Mike! We had a row last night! You said some very hurtful things ..." I'd stared at him, "What did you think was going to happen? Did you think I would wake you at the crack of dawn with a kiss, a cup of tea, a 'good morning sweetheart' and a quick fumble beneath the duvet ... as some sort of an *apology* to you?"

"Perhaps if you had then none of this would have happened ..."

"So last night's row and this morning's fiasco was *my* fault ...?"

"I didn't say that ..." he'd shaken his head, "I don't know why we are having this conversation in the hall ... go and put your feet up, sweetheart and I'll bring through some coffee; I made it fresh not ten minutes ago."

I'd nodded in defeat, already knowing that my words would prove to be nothing more than a pathetic and futile attempt to regain some ground.

"Okay, coffee's probably a good idea. We need to talk, Mike ..."

"I know ..." he'd responded cheerfully as he'd turned away from me towards the kitchen, "You

# The Runner – Part 1 Nicky's Story

have no idea of how much coffee I've already consumed today!"

"Yeah I do," I'd murmured to myself as I'd sunk into my favourite armchair, "You needed to be sober to plan your attack ..."

He'd brought the coffee in, handing me a mug as he'd passed me to sink into the corner of the sofa nearest to my chair, watching me as he'd raised his cup to his lips.

"Mike ..." I'd begun hesitantly.

"I thought it might be nice if we went out to dinner tonight," he'd interrupted, "I've booked us a table at the little restaurant by the Marina ..."

My heart had sunk; I hated Indian food. The spices never seemed to agree with me, sending me to the little boys' room for much of the following day and as I'd been neither fired nor suspended, Lou was expecting me at work tomorrow ... to host two shows! I'd seen the small smile on Mike's lips as he'd taken in my expression; one which I'd been too late to straighten to express my delight.

"That'll be nice ..." I'd said weakly.

"I thought so too," he'd agreed, "We don't do it often enough."

"No ..."

"I made Ricardo promise to give us your favourite table in the corner ..."

"Ricardo?" I'd raised my eyebrows, "You've booked a table at Ricardo's?"

"Yes ... and I've told him to make sure that he has your favourite white ... and not to try and fob

# The Runner – Part 1 Nicky's Story

us off with that 'house' shit of his like he tried to do the last time he hadn't got yours."

I'd seriously doubted that Ricardo would even remember us now since the last time we'd been was almost a year ago when Mike had relented to take me for my February birthday. Still, Mike's name and his bank balance was rather better known so perhaps those facts alone had indeed been enough to secure my preferred table in the corner at short notice and my favourite Fiano on ice.

I'd gaped at him stunned, "You did that; for me?"

He'd chuckled, "He'll be running to the wine merchant's if he hasn't got it ... that or it's being couriered over from Italy as we speak!"

"But ... you hate Italian food ..."

"I might but you don't ... and you love Ricardo's."

"You've booked a table at Ricardo's ... just for me?"

"I wouldn't do it for anyone else, sweetheart," he'd smiled, "And it's a small sacrifice to pay if it puts a smile on your face."

"But ... why?" I'd asked, "It's not my birthday and it's not our anniversary ..."

"I love you," he'd said, "Does there have to be any reason other than that?"

"But ... I still don't understand; why now; why tonight?"

"Gracious, Nicky; you're beginning to make it sound as if you don't *want* to go!" he'd said lightly,

"Ricardo's is one of the finest Italian restaurants in the South East ... still," he'd shrugged, "If you'd rather I cancelled ..."

"No! Of course I want to go ..."

"Well, good; stop looking for a motive, Nicky; there isn't one. I just want you ... want *us* ... to have an enjoyable evening ... that's all."

I'd regarded him carefully, searching for the lie but had been unable to find it. His expression had remained impassive and he'd continued to smile.

"I ... I don't know what to say; thanks."

"You're welcome," he'd said softly, leaning forward to set his mug down on the coffee table and patting the empty space next to him, "Come and sit beside me ..."

I'd hesitated but for a moment before I'd risen from my chair to do as he'd bid. His smile had broadened as his hand had reached out to cup my chin, his soft, warm lips meeting mine with the gentlest of kisses.

"You deserve a night out, Angel," he'd whispered, "You work far too hard ..."

"I like my work," I'd said, feeling my shoulders stiffen; certain that another row was brewing.

"I know you do ..." he'd retrieved his coffee mug and had casually sat back to settle into the corner of the sofa, "I'm sorry, sweetheart. I interrupted you. Weren't you going to say something?"

"What? ... I ... oh; yes," I'd sucked in a deep breath, blowing it out slowly and gently through my

## The Runner – Part 1 Nicky's Story

lips in an attempt to stem the rising tide of anxiety for a conversation I had known we must have but had little heart for, " Mike; we really do have to …"

"Oh! Before I forget …!" he'd sat up suddenly almost spilling and choking on his coffee in his eagerness to get the words out. My heart had sunk for the second time as he'd rushed on, "But I called the travel agent just before you called me … we're going away for the weekend."

"Going away?"

He'd been beaming at me, "I thought at first Paris or Rome; well, they're amongst the most romantic cities in the world … but at such short notice, I wasn't sure that you'd be able to get the time off work for a long weekend. I decided that it was hardly worth the flight … so I've booked us a weekend break in London."

"London?" I'd raised my eyebrows, "I *work* in London, Mike …"

"Well yes, I know," he'd said sounding a little disgruntled, "But I thought the most important thing was that we would be able to get away from home and spend some quality time together … I thought you'd think so too."

"Yes of course; that sounded most ungrateful of me … I'm sorry."

I'd bitten my lip, struggling to drum up some enthusiasm. I couldn't think of *anywhere* in the world in which I would want to spend a weekend with Mike. Home at least provided some sort of routine which enabled us to pretend that we still had a relationship; the weekly shop, the washing,

# The Runner – Part 1 Nicky's Story

the ironing; almost three hours of blissful silence whilst he read the Sunday papers. A weekend away would only peel off the paper covering the cracks, revealing them to be as wide as any gorge; wouldn't it?

"I know it's not Paris but you'll see Nicky; it will be just as romantic ..."

I'd doubted his assertion of romance but had thrown him a weak smile in response, "It's a very ... sweet gesture, Mike. Thank you."

"We have a full programme ..."

"Programme?" *Yeah Mike; so romantic. You've just made it sound like an executive weekend.*

"The agent has booked us tickets for the aquarium: the London Eye: Madame Tussauds: the Tower of London ..." My eyes had widened as he'd rattled it all off whilst a small smile had played around his lips as he'd watched me. He'd been playing me, distracting me from my purpose and we'd both known it, "... and a river cruise up to Windsor - we'll be having lunch on board by the way - and then of course, there's the theatre too on Saturday evening."

"Wow; it sounds ... brilliant."

"It will be," his smile had widened and I'd been sure that my flat tone confirming for him that he had been successfully wrong-footing me once more had been the reason for it, "I'm sorry Angel; I interrupted you ... again! You wanted to say something ..."

"What?"

"There was something you wanted to say ... before."

"Oh ... er, yes, I ..." I'd sat up a little straighter, momentarily closing my eyes to summon up the courage I'd needed, "Mike; we have to ..."

"Nicky; sorry ..." he'd said; neither looking nor sounding in the least apologetic for having cut me off mid-sentence for the third time, "You're *not* disappointed are you; that it's London I've chosen ...? I mean, if you'd rather we flew to Paris or Rome ..."

"Huh? Oh ... no; of course not," I'd said weakly, "I wasn't expecting to go anywhere; you've rather taken the wind out of my sails that's all. London will be ... nice."

He'd raised his eyebrows, "Just ... *nice?*"

I'd fought for my smile and lighter tone, "It'll be wonderful, Mike."

"So you're happy?"

"Yes, of course I am."

"You're looking forward to it?"

"Can't wait ..."

"Well luckily you haven't got to wait long," he'd leaned towards me and had kissed my lips, "And you won't have to do a thing. I'll do all the packing tomorrow, so all *you* will have to do is relax."

"Thanks ..."

"So; what were you going to say?"

"Oh! Erm ..."

# The Runner – Part 1 Nicky's Story

Somehow, the words I'd been rehearsing in my head on my train journey home had seemed to be rather futile now. Did they even matter? If they had I would have refused a weekend trip purporting love and romance; wouldn't I? To London or anywhere else. *Yes, Nicky; of course they matter. A weekend break is merely the sticking plaster.*

"Mike ..." I'd begun, "I really appreciate that you're doing all of this for me and I don't want to sound ..."

"Oh! There was one more thing ..." his hand had patted my leg.

My head had fallen against the back of the sofa and I'd closed my eyes in defeat, "Go on ..."

"Well, there's little point in you travelling all the way home on Friday just to have to travel all the way back up to London again," he'd said, "You'd be exhausted before the weekend even begins. So I thought it would make more sense if you were to meet me at the hotel once you've finished work ..."

I'd nodded, "That would make perfect sense ..." I'd opened my eyes again and had forced a smile, "You've thought it all out very well, Mike ..."

"I've tried to."

"I really don't know what to say ..."

"You don't have to say anything. I love you, Nicky," he'd whispered, taking my mug from my hands and setting it down on the table before pulling me into his arms, "I just want you to be happy ..." he'd murmured as he'd carried me down into a long, sweet and gentle kiss. He'd smiled when

## The Runner – Part 1 Nicky's Story

he'd finally let me up for air, "Hey! I did it again, didn't I?"

"Did what?"

"Butt in just as you were going to say something ..."

I'd felt my smile slip, "Yes, I was ..."

"Well?" he'd asked as he'd gently run his hand across my head to smooth down my hair, "What was it you wanted to say? I promise; I won't interrupt again ... my lips are sealed!"

He'd pinched his lips together, just as Lou had pinched mine together in the canteen yesterday. I'd smiled weakly at his gesture. Somehow it wasn't nearly as amusing as it had been when Lou had done it to me. I'd rolled over ... again and had allowed Mike to successfully goad me into silence with the promise of treats in much the same way as a man trained his puppy into obedience.

Shit! How could I speak now when I'd already lapped up the treats with my thanks and the sharing of kisses and caresses which I'd known were leading to the bedroom; my participation in such affection being my consent to follow him wherever he chose to lead me.

*You fucking idiot, Nicky!* It was too late now, I'd told myself. Mike had employed his strategy well and in so doing had rendered me powerless to defend myself in any row which might follow. In the last few minutes, he had acted to perfection the part of being the most caring, thoughtful and loving boyfriend a man could wish for. As his audience I had applauded him ... with the promise of a standing ovation 'somewhere a little more comfortable' on the cards.

"Sweetheart?" he'd prompted me; a small smile playing out on his lips, his eyes bright and looking amused.

"Nothing," I'd shaken my head, "I just wanted to say I'm sorry …"

## Chapter Six

I'd emerged from the bathroom fully dressed and had crept silently from the dark bedroom in my efforts not to awaken Mike. I'd wandered down the hallway and into the kitchen in my semi-comatose state, feeling exceedingly tired, thoroughly miserable and still reeling from the events of the previous evening. All the words I'd rehearsed in my head on the train home; the words which would have told my boyfriend that I'd finally had enough and was leaving him, were wasted now. I'd gone to Ricardo's defeated in the first battle but still with the hope of winning the war; a hope that my pathetic puppy-dog self had thwarted. Mike had played his ace card; one I hadn't been expecting and a scenario for which I'd had no script, much less a rehearsal and so I'd uttered the standard line. As a result of having done so, I would now have to face not only the consequences of my cowardice but I'd have to face Lou too.

I'd thought I was going to have a heart attack when I'd entered the kitchen to find him sitting at the breakfast bar. He'd turned his head towards me; a smile on his lips which spoke of victory.

"Jesus, Mike!" I'd gasped, my hand flying up to cover my heart, "You scared the crap out of me. I'd thought you were still in bed!"

He'd raised his eyebrows, "You didn't smell the coffee?"

"No." I hadn't ... just as I hadn't last night.

## The Runner – Part 1 Nicky's Story

"I've made you some toast," he'd said, pulling out the chair beside him and sliding a cup of coffee and a plate of toast towards me.

"Mike; it's half past four in the morning. You know it's too early for me to eat," I'd said, "I appreciate the coffee and whilst I appreciate the toast, I really can't face it; not at this hour. I'll get something at work."

His expression had darkened and he'd held a slice of the toasted bread in front of my mouth. "Eat it!" he'd ordered me.

After the smallest hesitation, I'd reluctantly opened my mouth, "Thanks." It had been like chewing on cardboard.

"That's better …" he'd nodded and the smile had appeared again, "So; what have you got to tell Louise today?"

I'd choked down the cardboard and had sighed. "I have to ask her if I can take Monday off."

"No," he'd shaken his head, "You *tell* her, Nicky; you don't *ask*."

"Mike …"

"Would you prefer that *I* call her and tell her?"

"No …"

"Well then; make sure that you do it as I'm going to make a call this morning and get us that appointment."

"Perhaps they won't have one; Monday *is* rather short notice, Mike."

## The Runner – Part 1 Nicky's Story

He'd smiled, "How many times do I have to tell you that it's not *what* you know that counts, Nicky but rather *who* you know?"

His words sufficient to have put the fear of God in me, I hadn't bothered to ask him the *'who'* or *'how'*; that he did was enough and nor did I doubt him. Whoever it was would no doubt manage to accommodate Mike at a time of *his* choosing and in so doing would help me to completely ruin my life quicker than I was doing it for myself.

His smile had broadened when I'd changed the topic.

"Why are you up so early anyway?"

"You woke me up ..."

"I'm sorry; I tried not to disturb you."

He'd shrugged, "Perhaps fortunate for you that you did."

"What do you mean?"

"It's raining cats and dogs," he'd said evenly, "I'll run you to the station."

"You don't need to do that ... I'm used to walking."

It was true. I *was* used to the daily walk to and from the station and I had been for more than two years; ever since my little Ford Fiesta had given up the ghost and Mike had declared that to buy another was a waste of money, regardless that it was my money I would have been wasting. *"I'll add you to my insurance as a named driver, Nicky,"* he'd said. He had and it had turned out to be an equal waste of money since I'd never been allowed to use

# The Runner – Part 1 Nicky's Story

his car. Eventually I had accepted the situation for what it was; the rows over the notion of a car of my own had not been worth the angst.

"I'll take you," he'd said firmly, "And I'll pick you up tonight too."

"Thank you. I'd appreciate the lift this morning," I'd answered, "But I really would prefer to walk home. If the train should be late ..." *God forbid that I should miss it.*

"I'll wait; no arguments, Nicky," he'd smiled, "In fact, I'll pick you up each evening from now on."

I'd frowned, "Why?"

"Is there any reason why I shouldn't?" he'd asked mildly.

His words had seemed to be questioning my fidelity and I'd turned my head to look at him more carefully. He'd raised his eyebrows and I'd felt my cheeks beginning to warm as I'd recalled the dream that the alarm clock placed beneath my pillow had so rudely interrupted; a beautiful dream which had caused me to dive into the shower where my well-practised wrist action and a few grunts and groans had finally broken the spell and brought the dream to an end. Had Mike heard me perhaps; or had I been talking in my sleep as I'd dreamt of my student? If such dreams counted as infidelity then I was indeed guilty. *Thank fuck I don't know his name!*

Aware that I'd been silent for a little too long, I'd finally shaken my head; "No, of course not," I'd said as I'd slid out of my chair, taking the crockery

## The Runner – Part 1 Nicky's Story

with me to load it into the dishwasher, "Just don't blame me whenever the train is late."

"Call me when it is and there will be nothing to blame you for," he'd said evenly, glancing up at the kitchen clock, "Well; time to go."

The journey to the station had been a silent one and whilst such silence with Mike usually had me on edge, I'd actually been grateful to him for not trying to press me into conversation. He'd only spoken once he'd stopped in front of the station entrance.

"Have a good day, Angel. Don't forget I'll be here to pick you up."

"Mike ... you really don't need to."

"I know ... but I'll be here just the same."

I'd nodded in defeat, "Okay; I'll see you later."

"See you later."

I'd climbed out of the car and had been about to close the door when he'd called out to me.

"Nicky; haven't you forgotten something?"

I'd hoisted my laptop bag higher onto my shoulder and had patted down my pockets. I'd shaken my head.

"No; I don't think so."

"A kiss, Nicky ...?"

"Oh; sorry," I'd murmured and had leaned back into the car to dutifully give him the kiss.

# The Runner – Part 1 Nicky's Story

"Don't forget to tell Louise," he'd reminded me as I'd closed the door and he'd wound down the electric window.

"I won't but what if ..."

"There is no 'what if', Nicky," he'd said serenely, "You're telling her remember; not asking ..."

"She could fire me if the answer is 'no' and I don't turn up for work ..."

"She won't fire you ..." he'd said confidently. I'd snorted and he'd laughed, "I promise you; she won't fire you ... that would be too easy."

I'd frowned, "What do you mean?"

"I want you to quit and you've refused. She hates me; has been trying to turn you against me almost from the beginning," he'd shrugged, "If she fires you now then I've won and she's lost."

"What?"

"I know you're on a little ego trip with the offer of Terry Jacks' show, sweetheart," he'd said spitefully, "But believe me; the only reason your precious Lou has offered it to you is to take you further away from *me*."

Without another word, he'd wound the window up and driven away, leaving me to watch as the car had disappeared around the one way system.

I'd sat on the train close to tears and feeling sick to the pit of my stomach. Was that all I really was to Mike now; some prize to be won at the end of a competition? Was that what last night's outing to Ricardo's had really been about? If so, it seemed to

## The Runner – Part 1 Nicky's Story

me that Mike had already won. But what had he won? Where did I rank in terms of prizes; first ... or the booby prize?

*Oh dear God, Nicky; what have you done?*

I'd still been brooding when my student had boarded at Clapham Junction. Given the relatively early hour, I'd been surprised to see him enter my carriage where for the briefest of moments our eyes had met. He'd seemed to hesitate before he'd turned his back against me and had begun to walk away through the full length of the carriage where he'd pulled the connecting door to the next open and disappeared through it. Stupid though it might have been, it had hurt that he hadn't even spared me the small acknowledgement he'd thrown my way yesterday.

I hadn't seen him leave the train at Victoria, nor had I seen him board the tube to Westminster. In fact, I hadn't even realised I'd still been looking for him until I'd boarded my final train on the Jubilee line to find him already leaning against the doors on the opposite side from where I'd entered the carriage. Our eyes had met for a second time and I'd bitten my lip, uncertain as to whether I should smile, speak or ignore him altogether.

His almost whispered, shy 'hi' had been all it had taken for my heart to begin to beat faster and my spirits to soar. My day had started out crap and I hadn't expected that it would get much better; not when I still had to face Lou, never mind what would be waiting for me back at home. Still; that one small word had been enough to put a spring in my step as I'd alighted at Waterloo one stop later.

## The Runner – Part 1 Nicky's Story

"See you ..." I'd ventured when I'd realised he wasn't disembarking.

He'd nodded and the small smile had almost become a grin, "Sure too ..."

**oOo**

"Bloody hell, Nicky!" Judy had pouted at me through the mirror; the dampened make-up sponge in one hand and the pot of concealer in the other, "You look bloody awful!"

"Thanks ..." I'd said drily.

"Well you do," she'd said heartlessly, "Aren't you sleeping?"

"I didn't sleep too well last night," I'd admitted, my left hand rising to rub away the gritty sleep I could still feel in the corners of my eyes.

"Oh dear! Did you and Mike have another ..." suddenly the sponge and the pot of concealer had landed on the dressing table in front of me as she'd shrieked; startling everyone in make-up, including me. She'd pulled my hand roughly away from my eyes to examine it, "Is that ..." her eyes had met mine, "Is that what I *think* it is?"

I'd glanced at the platinum ring with its overstated black, oval onyx surrounded by the flawless diamonds as its centrepiece and had smiled weakly, fighting back the heavy sigh threatening to leave my lungs.

"Mike took me out to dinner last night ..." I'd said, "The last thing I'd been expecting was for him

## The Runner – Part 1 Nicky's Story

to propose. It was rather a late night ... and I found it hard to settle. Probably all the excitement ..."

"Oh my God!" Judy had gasped as she'd begun to bounce around in front of my chair, "You're engaged?" she'd squealed, "Oh my God; Nicky! You're *engaged!*"

"Yes, I know," I'd said, my delighted smile in the mirror looking false even to me, "I was there ..."

"Oh my! He doesn't do things by half your Mike; does he?" she'd said, examining the ring more closely, "It's beautiful ... and so obviously expensive it's almost crude!"

"Thanks ..." I'd said, trying to pull my hand away on account of her exuberance causing curious faces to begin to turn in our direction. Judy hadn't finished her examination however and she'd gripped my hand more firmly to peer closely at the ring.

"White gold?"

"Platinum ..." I'd said dully, "Though it could just as easily be silver plate and I wouldn't know the difference."

"Heathen! Platinum huh?" she'd said, her tone almost one of awe, "Oh my! And just *look* at those stones," she'd chuckled, "they're *not* cubic zirconia by the way!"

I'd thrown her a small smile, "I've seen them ... and I know."

"Mike must *really* love you!"

"Yeah; I guess this is the proof huh?" I'd asked, my sarcasm seemingly floating over her head as she'd nudged my shoulder playfully.

# The Runner – Part 1 Nicky's Story

"You're a perfect bitch, Nicky Ashton; to have captured the heart of a man who buys you stuff like this! My God! It must be worth *thousands*!"

"Probably ..." I'd said evasively.

I hadn't actually known but Mike had said enough last evening to have actually cheapened it for me and if that hadn't done the job, his words to me just before he'd pulled away from the kerb this morning most assuredly had.

"God, I'm so jealous; I hate you ...!" Judy had said, her tone teasing, her eyes suggesting that there had been a hint of truth in her words.

I'd raised my eyebrows and had pulled my hand away, "Isn't that a little shallow? Shouldn't love be about something rather more than money and expensive jewellery?"

"Of course it should," she'd said, looking suitably chastised, her lips erupting into a huge grin moments later, "But if my boyfriend bought me something like that I wouldn't object! I'd have no problem at all loving him ... in any way he wanted and for however long!"

"You're a mercenary bitch, Judy," I'd said lightly, "I pity your fella if you should ever meet a man with a bank balance the size of Mike's. Does Todd know that you're likely to break his heart?"

"I won't break his heart," she'd said airily, "I'll keep him as my bit-on-the-side ... he's too damned good between the sheets for me to let him go completely!"

I'd forced a laugh, not liking her much more than I'd liked Mike, "Get on with your job, witch and rid me of these suitcases under my eyes ... I'm on in thirty minutes!"

She'd kissed my cheek, "Seriously darling; congratulations!"

"Thanks ..."

"I'm so glad that you and Mike have managed to iron out your differences. I take it that your little 'problem' in the bedroom department has been resolved too?"

"Mind your own business!" I'd said, feeling the heat beginning to burn my cheeks, "I'm never telling you anything *ever again*; you told Lou ..." I'd said accusingly, "I told you that in the strictest of confidence!"

"Hey! What do you think that chair is, Nicky; the therapist's couch?"

"Isn't it?"

"No; think of it as the hairdresser's chair ... and you know what terrible places salons are for gossip!" She'd nudged me playfully, "And before you say another word, Nicky Ashton, you've learned more than your fair share of gossip in that very chair."

"Humph ..."

"Don't bare it if you don't want to share it," she'd said lightly, "Your soul that is. It's the golden rule."

"Pity you didn't share *that* with me before I told you everything," I'd grumbled, "Still; I know not to do it again!"

She'd laughed, "Well, there are some things which simply have to be shared ..." she'd raised her voice to the room at large, "Hey everyone! Guess what? Our Nicky here is officially 'taken' ... you've *got* to come and see this!"

"Judy!" I'd chastised her crossly.

"What?" she'd raised her eyebrows, "It's not going to be a secret for long is it? Not with *those* rocks screaming for attention ... anyway; you must be bursting to share ... I know I would be!"

"We're not all as brash as you are, Judy!"

I'd endured five minutes of 'oohing' and 'aahing' over the ring where I'd smiled weakly and accepted congratulations, all the while feeling the weight of it on my finger, in my heart and around my neck.

**oOo**

"We've got high stock levels of this trio, Nicky," Beth, the floor manager fingered the necklace of the matching set which included a pair of earrings and a bracelet, "And limited on this one," she'd shown me another, "Can you make sure you showcase the first; make it your centrepiece this morning and really push it?"

"Sure; no problem. I'll highlight it as *'Nicky's deal of the day'*," I'd answered, adding a little sheepishly, "It's silver; right?"

"White gold and with a price to match," Beth had laughed, "Don't slip up or you'll never shift it!"

## The Runner – Part 1 Nicky's Story

I'd returned her laughter, "Whatever! At least I know the stones are sapphire," I'd said, picking up the bracelet and examining the stones carefully, "Sapphire is Carrie's birthstone and it's her favourite; especially these lighter shades. She had one of the lighter ones in her engagement ring although it was still a little different to these. I think she'd have liked this shade; it's almost lavender."

Beth had rolled her eyes, "You bloody heathen; they're tanzanite ... and I bet Carrie would know the difference!"

"Tanzanite; are they really?" I'd said, examining the stones more closely, "Never heard of it ... but it's very pretty."

Beth had handed me a set of prompt cards, "Here; take a good look at these and commit them to memory!"

"Yeah; think I'd better pay attention to the autocue too," I'd grinned as I'd skimmed through the cards, "I'm crap at this; jewellery really isn't my thing!"

"Perhaps it's not," she'd smiled at me, "But you're doing just fine and you certainly seem to be the viewers 'thing' ... although ..." Her smile had faded and she'd suddenly looked decidedly uncomfortable.

I'd frowned, not liking the sound of her 'although', "What is it, Beth?"

She'd bitten her lip and had sighed, "Christ, this is awkward."

"What is?"

# The Runner – Part 1 Nicky's Story

"Your ring," she'd said after a moment or two.

I'd glanced down at my finger, "What about it?"

"I've been told to tell you to take it off," she'd said, flipping through the sheets of paper pinned to her clipboard, unable to look at me.

"I'm sorry ...?"

"It's a little ... flashy," Beth's cheeks had filled with blood, "It could cause your assertion that you buy some of this stuff ..."

"I *do* buy some of this *stuff*, Beth; for Carrie ... as gifts from the kids; birthdays, Christmas ... Mother's day."

"I know but ... look; wearing that ring could cause your assertions to lose a little ... credibility; with the viewers."

I'd stared at her in disbelief, "Are you kidding me?"

"No," she'd shaken her head, "I'm sorry."

"You can't possibly be serious?"

"I'm sorry ..." she'd repeated.

"Jesus; you are! My God; I don't believe this! Would you ask me to take off my *watch*?" I'd asked a little affronted. In truth I'd hated my new ring as much as she'd seemed to but still; to tell me to take it off had been, in my opinion, a step too far.

"Hey! This isn't my idea, Nicky!" Beth had said indignantly, "This has come from above."

I'd raised my eyebrows, "From above?"

"The top ..."

# The Runner – Part 1 Nicky's Story

"I wasn't aware that any outside of make-up had seen it ... and I certainly haven't *told* anyone. I've been in my dressing room most of the morning."

"It seems that Judy managed to get a picture of it on her phone this morning ..."

Judy! I should have known. I hadn't bothered to ask Beth who it was that Judy had shown her phone to. I'd already known that too.

"And if I refuse to take it off ...?"

Beth had hesitated whilst she'd bitten down on her lip, "I've been told to take you off-air. I'm sorry, Nicky."

"I'll be taken off-air for wearing my *engagement* ring? You have *got* to be joking!"

"Just for this show, Nicky ..."

"I don't care. It's hardly the point," I'd said irritably, "It sounds like discrimination ..."

She'd laughed humourlessly, "You can bet your life they'll have an opt-out clause for that ..." she'd sighed, "Look; just take it off for this show, Nicky and you can have the post mortem afterwards."

"No ..."

"Nicky, please ..." she'd glanced at her watch, "I'm running out of time ... and you're out of options."

"I won't be intimidated," I'd said firmly, shaking my head, "It's an empty threat."

## The Runner – Part 1 Nicky's Story

"I don't think so. The boss is adamant that it is way too flash for this show ..." Beth had shaken her head, "I'm sorry, Nicky. It's your call."

A movement in the gallery above the studio had caused me to look up to see that Louise, her lips set in a thin line and her arms folded across her chest, had been watching the short exchange between me and the floor manager.

Beth had suddenly tugged at her microphone, pulling it down from where it had been tucked up above her headset.

"One minute, Nicky," she'd said, "Johanna's on standby to anchor this one; so, I need your decision. Are you going to take off your ring?"

I'd hesitated, knowing that Mike would probably be watching this morning and it was highly unlikely that he wouldn't notice if his ring wasn't in clear view. It had seemed to me that whatever I chose to do, a row was heading my way. I was damned if I did and damned if I didn't. I'd pushed my earpiece into my ear. What could they possibly do once we were live? I'd glanced at my monitor to see that in the smaller studio next door, Johanna too was adjusting her earpiece for comfort. The live feed could be switched from my camera to camera three in a heartbeat.

"Nicky?" Beth had prompted me, "What's it to be?"

My eyes had once more met those of Louise's, still watching me from the windows of the gallery whilst Rob had begun the countdown in my ear.

## The Runner – Part 1 Nicky's Story

*"Twenty seconds; standby everybody ... Nicky!"* Rob's voice had suddenly whispered into my ear, *"I know the deal, mate ... and that witch has the power to make or break a career. I won't risk mine for insubordination ... don't risk yours either. It's not worth it. Camera one standby; camera three, standby; roll titles ... Nicky!"* Rob had hissed into my ear, *"She isn't fucking kidding mate. Make your decision before I'm forced to make it for you; and in ten, nine, eight ... Nicky standby; Johanna standby ... in five, four ... Nicky! ... two ..."* I'd slipped the ring from my finger into my pocket. *"One ... camera one, we're live!"*

I'd already been delivering my spiel into the camera when Rob had delivered his apologies into my ear and Louise had turned on her heel and left the gallery.

*"Nicky; Louise says I am to let you know that she can't do lunch today ..."*

Well; I'd supposed that at least I'd known what she'd thought of my cowardice.

**oOo**

I'd been barely one hundred yards from the studio building when the young man had run headlong into me almost knocking me clean off of my feet and taking my breath away with him; in more ways than one. He'd been talking into his iPhone whilst simultaneously trying to remove a brown padded envelope from his rucksack.

## The Runner – Part 1 Nicky's Story

"Oh hell; I'm so sorry ..." he'd mumbled, pulling the phone away from his ear and bending towards the package which had tumbled out of his bag and onto the ground.

I'd got there first; scooping up the package which had been about the size and weight of a DVD and had held it out to him, trying to surreptitiously read the address label as I did so, in the hope that it would give me a clue as to not *its* destination but his. He'd straightened up and had looked a little startled when he'd recognised me.

"Oh! It's you!"

I'd laughed, "Yes; me again!"

"I really *am* sorry. Are you okay?"

"Hey; no worries ... and I'm fine. Here ..." I'd held the package out to him.

"Thanks," he'd taken the padded envelope into his hand and had thrown me a shy smile before pasting the phone to his ear once more. "I'm really sorry ..." he'd whispered before hurrying on his way, already speaking into his phone; "Yes; I'm here now."

"Oh, sure; no harm done," I'd said, even though I'd known he wouldn't hear. As if in a dream, I'd turned to watch him, surprised to see him pulling open the doors of my own building.

I'd stood on the pavement, biting on my lip and wondering what he could possibly be doing inside of the studio building. My heart had picked up its pace as the erratic thoughts had struck me; *perhaps he isn't a student ... perhaps he works there. Oh my God! I could have been sharing the*

# The Runner – Part 1 Nicky's Story

*same building with him! Perhaps if I wait outside long enough, I will see him leave and then perhaps I will be able to speak to him.*

My stomach had suddenly growled, bringing me sharply to my senses and reminding me that I was supposed to be going in search of a sandwich!

*Jesus, Nicky; what's wrong with you? Get a grip! He's probably meeting someone for lunch; after all, didn't you hear him say, 'I'm here now'? Yes; he smiled at you and he whispered 'hi' this morning but ... he's bound to be attached and quite apart from anything else he's probably straight ... and even if he* is *gay and unattached, why the hell would he be interested in you? Oh yes; and one other thing, Nicky Ashton ... you've just promised Mike that you'll marry him!*

With this last morose thought, I'd turned my steps towards Waterloo station and the coffee shop on the station concourse. It wouldn't solve any of my problems but a caffeine hit would be welcome just the same. Having spent almost fifteen minutes deliberating all that the chiller cabinet had to offer, I'd finally selected a ham salad sandwich and had taken it to the counter where I'd heard myself muttering the words *four shot tall latte* for which I'd received a look of horror from the Barista in return.

"*Four* shots, sir? Are you sure?"

I wasn't but God, it was tempting ... and the protagonist in my book seemed to be getting by quite well on it!

"Four shots will probably give you a heart attack ..." the voice had said quietly beside me, "but if you promise to make it just *one* extra shot ... it'll be on me."

It hadn't really been necessary for me to turn my head towards the speaker; I'd committed his voice and the soft lisp to memory ever since I'd first heard it on the short train journey between Victoria and Clapham Junction. He'd smiled coyly when I'd raised my eyebrows.

"It's an apology," he'd said as he'd pulled out his wallet and opened it to remove his bank card, "For almost knocking you off your feet ... and it's also a 'thank you'; for picking up the parcel I dropped."

"Thanks," I'd returned his smile, "But you don't need to buy my coffee ..."

"I'd like to ..."

I'd hesitated but for a second before I'd confirmed my order for the Barista, "A tall latte please ... with one extra shot."

## Chapter Seven

"So; is this where I'm supposed to use the tacky phrase *'we really shouldn't keep meeting like this'*?" he'd asked lightly, his tone one of amusement as he and I had left the coffee shop together, our coffees in paper cups covered with plastic lids.

I'd laughed, "We do seem to keep bumping into each other don't we?"

"Quite literally ..." he'd smiled warmly at me; a smile sufficient to have made me feel weak at the knees.

"Where were you heading?" I'd asked.

He'd shrugged, "Back to the office I suppose. You ...?"

I'd resisted the urge to raise my eyebrows when he'd mentioned that he had an office to return *to* since his attire didn't seem to fit that of a city office.

"I was going to take a walk down to the river bank if you wanted to ... I mean ..." I'd felt my cheeks beginning to burn. I hadn't a clue how I was supposed to do this without sounding as if I was trying to pick him up, "If you have the time ..."

"Sure," he'd said amiably, "It's a pleasant enough day; for January."

"Hmmm," I'd murmured, "It always seems to feel warm when the sun is bright." I'd thrust my hand out towards him, "I'm Nicky by the way; Nicky Ashton."

## The Runner – Part 1 Nicky's Story

He'd secured the rucksack slung over his shoulder and had switched his coffee cup from his right hand to his left.

"Aaron ..."

I'd smiled, "Pleased to meet you, Aaron ..."

"Ditto ..."

"Do you usually have lunch in your office?" I'd asked as we'd left Waterloo and set off towards the riverbank.

He'd smiled, "Not very often; no."

"Where is your office?"

"Westminster ..." he'd said, sipping at his coffee, "What about you; where do you work?"

"I work in the building you were heading for ..."

"Oh really; what do you do?"

"I work for a shopping channel."

"As ...?"

I'd smiled at him, "I'm a presenter ..."

He'd raised his eyebrows before throwing me an apologetic smile, "I'm sorry; I wouldn't have known. I don't watch any of those channels ..."

I'd laughed, "Don't apologise; I promise you that my ego is still intact ..."

"Well good ... although you don't strike me as the egotistical type."

"Thank God for that," I'd chuckled, "Believe me; I'm no Princess. There are more than enough of

## The Runner – Part 1 Nicky's Story

those in my business without me adding to the count."

He'd smiled and had rolled his eyes in a manner which had made my heart miss another beat, "Oh God! Tell me about it ..."

I'd stolen a glance at him, "That sounded rather ... knowledgeable."

"It's not knowledge exactly," he'd said serenely, "My degree is in Television and Media; I came across the *type* in my third year."

My jaw had almost dropped to the floor and Lou's words of yesterday had returned to me in an instant; *perhaps it's fate ...*

"You're kidding?" I'd heard my sharp intake of breath, "You work in television too?"

He'd laughed, "I said that my *degree* was in Television and Media; not that I work in television!"

"Oh!" I'd felt my cheeks beginning to burn; a burn which had been completely unrelated to the cold sting of the January air.

"I like it when your cheeks do that," he'd said shyly, "It makes you look cute."

The burn in my cheeks had deepened, "Cute?"

Suddenly his face had flamed red too, causing me to imagine that in our cheeks at least we must have made a pretty convincing pair of book ends. Of course it had provoked the obvious question; *is he gay?* He had to be didn't he? Why else would one guy tell another that he was *'cute'?* And yet, he'd looked sorely embarrassed.

"Healthy then ..." he'd offered.

## The Runner – Part 1 Nicky's Story

I'd smiled, "I rather liked 'cute' ..."

My attempt to fish had provided me without the bite I'd been hoping for as he'd made no response, choosing instead to sip at his coffee. Perhaps it had been nothing more than a poorly chosen word spoken in all innocence; after all, it wasn't as if he'd placed any emphasis upon it, was it?

"So; how long have you been a presenter?" he'd asked, pulling me from my musings.

"Getting on for ten years now ... although I've only been an anchor for these past fourteen months. I fell into presenting quite by accident," I'd smiled at him, "I don't have your degree ... in fact, I don't even *have* a degree; three 'A' Levels but no degree."

"How so?"

I'd raised my eyebrows, "How come I don't have a degree?"

"No," he'd chuckled and had shaken his head, "I meant; how did you manage to fall into your career 'by accident'?"

"Oh, I see!" I'd laughed, "I was a shop assistant believe it or not."

"A shop assistant?" His tone had expressed interest rather than the scorn Mike had displayed when he'd learned of how I had begun my career.

I'd nodded, "I worked in a high-end department store; started working there at weekends whilst I was at college and then, whilst I was awaiting my exam results, a vacancy for departmental assistant

## The Runner – Part 1 Nicky's Story

manager arose. I was offered it and as it had prospects, I accepted ..." I'd smiled at him, "At that time, I rather liked having money in my pocket and I thought I'd infinitely prefer it to being a poor student!"

"Yeah; not much fun in that ... nor is the debt resulting from student loans!" He'd grinned at me, "Do you know; I actually sat and worked it out a few weeks ago. At my current rate, I'll be debt free in about thirty years!"

"Really?" I'd raised my eyebrows playfully, "That quick huh? I'm impressed! You *must* be doing well!"

"Well, perhaps not yet!" he'd laughed, "Anyway; you were telling me how you came to be a TV presenter ..."

"Oh, yes! Well, I worked in the shoe department and one day this woman walked in ... bit of a tricky customer to say the least," I'd said, recalling how Lou and I had met, "Anyway; she was a pain in the arse and she and the department manager nearly came to blows. He handed her over to me ... and eventually she left with not just the pair of shoes my boss had been unsuccessfully trying to sell her but another three pairs too ... and all with their matching handbags!" I'd shrugged, "She returned the next day to tell me that she had a proposition for me ... a decent one, I hasten to add ..." I'd smiled when Aaron had chuckled at my words, "... and then she invited me to lunch. I met her for lunch on my day off a few days later and that was when she told me that she was looking for a part-time presenter to fill in for holidays and sickness. Nobody was more surprised than me

## The Runner – Part 1 Nicky's Story

when she told me that she thought I'd be perfect in the role and invited me along to the studio for a screen test."

"Obviously you passed it ..."

"She called to offer me the job whilst I was still on the train home. The pay and benefits she was offering for part-time work weren't very much different to what I was getting at the store for full-time hours ... so of course, I accepted. It was still retail; just a different medium." I'd smiled at him, "So you see; I entered this world completely green. It was one hell of a steep learning curve believe me; trying to understand life in a studio; how it all worked ..."

He'd returned my smile, "I know. Of course, most of our *learning the ropes* as it were took place in the studios at Uni but it wasn't so very different to the real thing. Not quite as romantic as some imagine is it?"

"No," I'd agreed, "It's bloody hard work behind the scenes!" I'd thrown him another small smile, "So; if you're not in the industry ... what do *you* do?"

His phone had rung before he could answer and he'd pulled it out of his pocket to glance at the screen. He'd pulled a face and had groaned.

"What *now*?" he'd murmured before giving me an apologetic smile, "Excuse me a mo, Nicky; I have to take this."

I'd nodded understandingly, "Sure ..."

"Hi Baz ..." he'd taken a few steps away from me, leaving me to stare up at the London Eye; a

## The Runner – Part 1 Nicky's Story

crude reminder that in a couple of days I'd be aboard one of the capsules with Mike and that being so, I'd had no business to be engaged in small talk with this young man who had so captivated me; a conversation that at the end of which I'd secretly been hoping I would have obtained Aaron's number and given him mine.

"I'm so sorry, Nicky; I have to go ..." he'd said when he'd retraced his steps back to where I'd been waiting.

"Oh! Okay ..." I'd said evenly whilst trying to swallow my disappointment.

Had it been merely my imagination, or had he too looked disappointed when he'd offered me an explanation?

"Rush job's just come up ... I need to get back to the office."

I'd nodded, "Sure; no sweat. I understand ..."

He'd held his hand out to me, "It's been really nice to meet you ..."

"Yeah; you too," I'd said as we'd shook hands. I'd have preferred to have given and received a kiss on the cheek. His next words had made my heart sink.

"See you around ..."

Clearly he hadn't wanted to exchange numbers. If he had, he would have asked before running out on me; wouldn't he? The thought had prevented *me* from making the suggestion.

"Yeah ..."

## The Runner – Part 1 Nicky's Story

He'd watched me for a moment before throwing me the shy smile again, "Okay; well ... I'm outta here!"

"Yeah; me too," I'd said, jerking my thumb over my shoulder in the vague direction of the studio building, "I should be getting back anyway ..."

He'd taken a few steps backwards, "Take care then ..."

"Yeah; you too ..."

He'd nodded his head and had turned his back against me; leaving me to watch him walk away ... taking opportunity with him.

"Oh! Aaron; wait up!"

He'd stopped, looking at me enquiringly whilst he'd waited for me to catch up. I'd reached him and had dived into the pocket of my trousers to pull out some loose change.

"You bought my coffee ... for which I thank you ... but you paid for my sandwich too," I'd said awkwardly as I'd rummaged through the coins in the palm of my hand, "I think it was three-fifty ..." I'd held out four pound coins, "But that should cover it."

He'd stared at the coins in my hand before he'd shaken his head, "Thanks; but lunch was on me."

"Oh no; I couldn't ...!"

He'd smiled at my protest and I hadn't been able to help but feel the jolt of electricity which had run through me when he'd reached out to curl my hand closed over the coins, "Put your money away. It was my pleasure; honestly."

# The Runner – Part 1 Nicky's Story

"Oh; well ... thanks."

"You're welcome ..." he'd glanced at his watch, "I'm sorry; I really *do* have to go ..."

"Yeah; sure; of course you do ... sorry to have held you up."

He'd nodded and had turned away from me once more. I hadn't been sure which of us had been more surprised when he'd turned around again; me, to see that he had or him to find me still watching him.

"You really *do* look cute when you blush," he'd called to me; a grin lighting up his face, "See you ..."

I'd stared after his retreating back, stunned.

"Aaron! Wait!" He'd turned, his eyebrows raised in enquiry once more. "Will I see you again?" I'd called out to him.

"Of course!"

"When?"

He'd laughed, "When you follow me onto the wrong line again ..."

## Chapter Eight

"That was a dirty trick you played this morning," I'd said irritably, watching the woman as she'd risen from her desk to perch on it in front of me.

"It was a business decision, Nicky ..." she'd folded her arms across her chest and had shrugged indifferently.

"Bullshit Louise!" I'd retorted angrily, "You're pissed at me ... and that was your way of letting me know it! Your decision was *personal!*"

"Business ..." she'd repeated.

"You humiliated me!"

"Get used to it, sweetie," she'd said serenely, "I'm sure Mike will have plenty more lined up for you where that came from ..."

"You bitch!"

She'd raised her eyebrows, "I'll let that go, Nicky," she'd said evenly, "I understand you're upset ... but do please remember that you're in my office; in our *place of work* ..." she'd added pointedly. "I was forced to conduct one disciplinary yesterday; I really don't wish to conduct another today ... especially for you."

I'd sighed, "I'm sorry that you had to learn of it from Judy. I would have told you ..."

"But you didn't ..."

"No; I didn't get the chance."

# The Runner – Part 1 Nicky's Story

"You could have called me on your way in this morning."

I'd sighed for a second time, "Why are you so mad at me anyway?"

"Mad at you, Nicky?" she'd shaken her head, "Why would I be mad at you? It's not my place ..."

"You think I'm doing the wrong thing ..."

"Doing the *wrong* thing, Nicky?" she'd laughed, "You don't need me to tell you that ..."

"Mike and I had a real heart-to-heart last night ..."

"Did you?" she'd asked mildly, "And was that before or after he'd wooed you with the finest dining, roses and chocolates ... and dropped down onto one knee with a ring for which most people would have to take out a second mortgage?"

I'd swallowed, "He's rung you ..."

"No, of course he hasn't but nor did he need to. I know exactly how his type operates. Tell me, Nicky; amidst all the wooing, did he apologise for his abominable behaviour towards you ... or did you apologise to *him*; for not having been gracious enough to accept his vile treatment of you when it is he who pays for the comfortable roof over your head?"

I'd swallowed uncomfortably whilst she'd gazed at me with a mixture of pity and annoyance.

"I'd thought as much," she'd said drily reaching for my hand; her lips set in a tight line of barely concealed disgust as she'd looked at the ring on my finger whilst I had watched the monitor on the wall streaming the live feed of Tess Rogers presenting the new spring lines in female fashion.

"It's very pretty," she'd finally said, releasing my hand and pushing herself up from her perch on the edge of her desk and moving to sit behind it.

I'd swallowed, watching her looking thoughtful; disappointment etched in the strong features of her face as she'd picked up a pencil which had found its way between her teeth in a fluid but unconscious movement. Her eyes had met mine and the cheery smile upon her lips had been as false as mine had been in make-up.

"So; when are you leaving?"

She'd been the first not to utter the obligatory word of 'congratulations'. I'd been grateful that she hadn't but it had stung none the less; stung because it was the confirmation that she believed me to be all that I already knew for myself. I was a weak and spineless fool. Had it been anybody else but Lou …

I must have looked as confused as I'd sounded, "Leaving …?"

She'd shrugged, pointing her pencil towards the finger of my left hand, "Well; that's what *that* is, isn't it? Your notice …"

I'd frowned, "No …"

Lou had laughed, "Of course it is! Maybe not *immediately* but you don't honestly think Mike is going to allow you to continue working once you're married, do you?"

"He knows my career is important to me …"

# The Runner – Part 1 Nicky's Story

"I don't doubt it," she'd smiled, "But he'll rob you of it just the same ... and you'll let him."

"No I won't!" I'd denied hotly, "He and I talked about this last night ..."

"Really?" she'd asked, almost sneering at me, "And when you were talking to the brick wall, Nicky, did you happen to notice the writing upon it?"

I'd swallowed, "It's not like that ..."

"Isn't it?" she'd shaken her head, "Then what *is* it like, Nicky? Tell me ... because I don't get it. Two days ago you wanted to leave him; had virtually made your mind up that you would ... and now you've committed your life to the man. Two days ago you were telling me how he abuses you in the bedroom; how he controls everything you do and say; how he makes you feel like a sack of shit ... utterly useless and entirely without worth. Today you're defending him."

"He's been feeling insecure ... and that's my fault," I'd said, squirming in my seat beneath her raised eyebrows and the expression of disbelief, compelling me to rush on before she could speak, knowing I that was trying to defend myself rather than my new fiancé, "Mike sold the business so that we could spend more time together ... and I started to work more and more. Put yourself in his shoes Louise; what do you think that said to him?"

"That he was losing control ..." she'd said bluntly.

"I went from being a part-time, stand-in presenter to *anchor* in a daytime prime slot, Louise!"

# The Runner – Part 1 Nicky's Story

"Yes, you did ... and it took you eight years of bloody hard slog to prove yourself to get there. Mike should have been proud of you ... except he wasn't; was he? He resented your success ..."

"It came right at the time Mike was signing the paperwork to sell the business," I'd said, ignoring her, "Mike had thought that my acceptance of the promotion meant something that it didn't. He'd thought I'd taken the job as a means of spending *less* time with him ..."

She'd raised her eyebrows, her tone laden with sarcasm, "You mean you didn't ...? Oh, I'm sorry; my mistake ... I thought you had."

I'd rushed on with my pathetic defence as if she hadn't spoken, "He hadn't wanted me to accept it ... but I took it anyway ... and as he says; it wasn't as if we needed the money. He's right; I took it as a means of massaging my own ego ..."

"Oh my God, Nicky Ashton! Will you just listen to yourself; just for a moment! He's a control freak! He's not even here and he's controlling you ... pulling your strings and making you dance his tune! Even the words tumbling out of your mouth aren't yours ... they're *his!*"

"That's not true ..."

"Isn't it?" she'd said, "Alright then; prove it! Tell me that you're not going to turn down my offer; tell me that you're going to take Terry's slot. It's a good career move for you and you know it. So tell me you're not here to throw it all away!"

## The Runner – Part 1 Nicky's Story

I'd hung my head, watching myself twisting the ring around my finger, unable to meet her eye, "There'll be other opportunities ..." I'd said quietly.

She'd shaken her head, "No there won't; not for you. Mike will see to that ..."

"That's not fair, Louise! Mike *will* support me ... when the time is right; it's just not now."

"I'd thought so," she'd nodded her head, "You're turning me down."

"Jesus Lou! You're speaking as if I'm trying to personally offend you! I don't *want* to turn it down!" I'd fired at her, "It's just not the right time for me."

"It's not the right time for *Mike* you mean!" she'd fired back, sounding every bit as frustrated as she did irked, "And it will *never* be the right time for him ..." she'd tossed her pencil onto the table in her annoyance, "Oh whatever, Nicky!"

"It's not like that," I'd insisted, "This is my decision, not Mike's ..."

"Yeah, yeah ... if it makes it easier for you to believe that I'm buying into that notion, then fine!" She'd sat back in her chair and released a heavy sigh, "Perhaps you're right ... I need someone who is *hungry* for it. I thought that person was you but clearly I was wrong; I misjudged you ... you're not hungry enough."

"Louise!"

She'd pulled a pad towards her and had picked up the pencil she'd tossed aside, "Was there anything else?" she'd asked fixing a smile in place, "As you can see ... I'm rather busy."

# The Runner – Part 1 Nicky's Story

I'd bitten my lip. Mike had asked me last night to try and get off early on Friday as well as to take Monday off ... but given Louise's mood now, perhaps this wouldn't have been the best time to ask.

"What?" Louise had sounded frustrated.

"Well ..." Did I dare to further risk her wrath? On the other hand, Mike would know I was lying if I were to tell him that I *had* asked but unfortunately Louise couldn't spare me at such short notice. Besides; if I wasn't at his side on Monday, he would make damned *sure* that I had no job to return to on Tuesday.

"Oh for fuck's sake; whatever it is, Nicky ... spit it out!"

"Mike arranged a weekend break for us yesterday; a celebration of sorts."

She'd raised her eyebrows, "Oh my! Mike *was* a very busy bee after his little stunt yesterday ... dinner, a proposal, a weekend break ... he'd even managed to run out and buy you an over-the-top, extortionately expensive ring ..."

"No he didn't," I'd heard myself saying defensively, "He'd been planning to propose on Christmas Day ... except I wasn't at home; I was here. He'd commissioned the ring some months before ..."

"You weren't here on Christmas *night,* Nicky ... what was to stop Mike from making you a wonderful dinner; opening a bottle of bubbly and going down on one knee then?"

## The Runner – Part 1 Nicky's Story

"I've told you, Lou; things had been difficult between us. He'd imagined that my choosing to work meant I didn't love him anymore ..."

She'd snorted, "You pretty much told me on Tuesday that it was *precisely* for that reason you took all the shifts to fill the breach here ..."

I'd sighed, "Perhaps it would have been different had I just sat down and talked to him as I did yesterday ..."

"You mean that *he* talked to *you!*" she'd snorted derisively.

I'd ignored her. "If I had only done so then I'd have known we were each feeling the same ... that we'd just lost our way a little; that's all ... and we would have sorted matters out sooner. If only I had then what happened yesterday would never have happened ... it was my fault; not Mike's."

"And the rough sex; the sex where he's been physically hurting you ... that's been your fault too has it?" she'd asked drily.

"He was hurting ... he lost control; he couldn't help himself ..."

"Hurting? From all you've told me, I'd say he was *angry,* Nicky and I'd say he was angry because he knew he was losing control ... over you; at least in part. I'd say sex is some kind of a weapon to him ... one which he knows will hurt ... physically *and* emotionally. In your responses to such abuse, he's teaching you to disconnect ... from everything and everyone around you ... including *yourself,* Nicky!"

"He couldn't have been sweeter last night," I'd said, "He was so gentle, so considerate ..."

# The Runner – Part 1 Nicky's Story

"It won't last," she'd said tonelessly, "It never does with his sort. He'll woo you again ... for a while; until he's got you right where he wants you; until you've married him ... and then you'll be right back where you started; you mark my words, Nicky Ashton." She'd sighed, "Still; it's not for me to tell you how to live your life ... and you wouldn't listen anyway; not now. He's done a good number on you overnight ... and if you want to kid yourself otherwise ..."

I'd smiled weakly, "Perhaps it was six of one and half a dozen of the other ..." I'd suggested, "I think our wires became crossed and we were both afraid ..."

"Whatever! I really don't think I want to hear it, Nicky. I can't bear it. If you think that to be abused is acceptable; well ... nothing I say will change your mind," Lou had said wearily, "His timing has been impeccable whichever way *you* choose to look at it." She'd smiled, "I can't condone ... *that* ..." she'd pointed at my lead weight again, "Not when I know what it really means; as do *you,* however much you try to convince me otherwise ... although I think you're trying to convince yourself rather than me. Still; when you need a friend, Nicky ... well; I'm here for you. I always will be ..." she'd sighed again, "I'm going to give you some advice, sweetie; you won't like it but I'm going to give it to you anyway. Keep your eye on the ball, won't you? When Mike begins to separate you from your friends ... and he will ... then for God's sake! Know *that's* the time for you to wake up and smell the coffee because if you don't, you really *will* be in trouble ... and even I might not be able to help you."

# The Runner – Part 1 Nicky's Story

"Aren't you being a little melodramatic ...?"

"No," she'd said, harshly, "I speak from experience ..."

My eyes had widened in shock, "Experience ...?"

She'd smiled, "You didn't know that I'd been married, did you?"

"No ..."

"Well I was; to a man just like Mike. Like you, I knew he was a control freak and like you, I imagined that he was insecure; that if I married him all would turn out well. It didn't, Nicky. It went from bad to worse. He grew violent ... first it was the sex – forcing me to have it when I didn't want it, I mean - and then the hair-pulling and the punching started. He'd do it because I'd been late putting the dinner on the table; because he'd come home to find my best friend sitting on the sofa ... or because I'd been on the phone too long ... *with my Mother!*"

"I ... I'm sorry, Lou; I had no idea."

"I don't advertise the fact, Nicky." She'd sighed, "My career began to take off and his remedy for putting paid to it was having a baby; it was always the 'big one' back then; in terms of employers and women of my age. Opportunities were few since we were a risk; we tended to trot of on maternity leave to have our children and very often we didn't return, even though our jobs had to be held open for us. Still; I hadn't been in any rush. My career was everything to me at that time; to have a baby then would have been selfish ... but Mark was insistant; said it would make everything better between us. I wasn't ready but ... I got pregnant."

I'd raised my eyebrows, "You have a child?"

She'd shaken her head, "No. I lost the baby ... after Mark had tried to strangle me with my bra one night, rendering me almost unconscious; almost but not quite. He'd wanted me to feel every punch, every kick; wanted me to feel the life leaving the baby in my womb ..."

"Oh my God; Louise ...!"

She'd smiled sadly, "I lost the baby ... and I lost my womb with her ..."

My eyes had widened further in horror, "You lost ...?" I'd shaken my head in disbelief, unable to speak.

Louise had thrown me a wan smile, "Mark had walked out of the house after pushing me down the stairs, leaving me bleeding at the bottom; he'd even stepped over me to get to the door ... My friend found me two hours later. She'd come over when I hadn't answered the phone; her husband kicked the front door in ..."

"What happened to Mark? The police arrested him; right?"

"Oh yes; he was arrested," she'd agreed, "But in those days, the police didn't have the power to press charges for domestic violence; not without the victim to make a complaint. I didn't make one. I was too frightened of Mark to do that. The police knew it but there was nothing they could do. To all intents and purposes, I'd rendered them helpless ... me too really since to change my statement would have made me out to be a liar ... which of course I was ..."

"But you weren't!"

She'd smiled, "I meant that I hadn't told the truth when I'd said that Mark had done nothing to be held to account for. Had I changed my mind and told the real truth ... well; his defence lawyers would have wiped the floor with me," she'd shrugged, "I doubt that the Crown Prosecution Service would even have taken it to Court in the end. I wouldn't have been a credible witness."

"What about the baby? Surely he could have been charged with causing the baby's death?"

"Mark told them that I must have fallen down the stairs; running after him when he'd left following a row. I didn't disagree. He played the part of the grieving father-to be exceedingly well; even I'd almost believed him," she'd shrugged, "The baby's death was deemed to be the result of a tragic accident."

"Surely the medical evidence would have said different; he'd punched you; kicked you ..."

"It didn't matter ... not all the while I'd insisted that I'd got my injuries from falling top to bottom down the stairs ..."

"My God! Lou; I'm so sorry ..."

"I don't want you to be sorry for me, Nicky," she'd said earnestly, "I want you to learn from my mistakes ..."

"Mike's not like that ..."

## The Runner – Part 1 Nicky's Story

"Mike's exactly like Mark ..." she'd said, "If you marry him, Nicky ... well; you'll soon wish that you'd listened to the side of you that already knows; the part of you which already fears him."

"I don't fear him ..."

"Don't you?"

"No ..."

"Then tell him you're taking the job ..."

"I can't; I've told you ... it's not the right time. The kids are still so young for one thing ..."

"The kids don't live with you; you see them for a few hours every Saturday and have them for one weekend in four. You don't work weekends now and you still wouldn't be working at the weekend ..."

"No; but as Mike has pointed out ... I'm going to be far more tired working *two* slots ..."

She'd shrugged, "Fair enough; then take Terry's and I'll find someone else to do yours."

I'd bitten my lip, "It's tempting, I'll admit ... but I don't think so. Mike ..."

"Mike won't like it," she'd nodded, "It gives you too much exposure ..."

"No!" I'd protested, "It's not that at all! It's just that we don't have much time together now. Mike likes to dine out and by the time I get home and have read through my brief for the next day ... well; it's hardly worth the effort. If I take Terry's show, I'll never be home before midnight."

## The Runner – Part 1 Nicky's Story

We'd spent a few moments almost glaring at each other before she'd spoken again, her tone still weary.

"You wanted to ask me something? Something about a weekend break ...?"

I'd nodded, "Mike arranged it as a surprise. I wish that he'd asked me first but as he said; it wouldn't have been a surprise if he had ..."

Louise had understood, "You want some time off?"

"Yes; just the Friday afternoon ... which would mean me skipping the meeting after I come off-air ... and I'd need the whole of the Monday off too."

"Alright," she'd sighed, "When ...?"

I'd hesitated.

"*When,* Nicky?"

"This weekend ..."

Her eyes had widened, "*This* weekend? Christ Nicky; Mike doesn't do it by halves, does he ... trying to fuck your career up, I mean!"

"It's not often I ask you for anything Louise ..."

Her eyes had drifted towards the monitor on the wall where she'd watched the young presenter for a few moments. She'd shrugged as she'd returned her attention to me, "Whatever! By all means leave early on Friday and take Monday off too. I'm sure Tess will be only too glad to cover your arse ... she at least *is* hungry. I imagine she will be thrilled to take the crumbs from your table ..."

# The Runner – Part 1 Nicky's Story

Her words had been a stab to my chest. "Louise ..."

She'd smiled at me; the smile of my boss rather than my dear and close friend, "Was that everything?"

I'd bitten my lip whilst she'd gazed steadily back at me, "Yes ..."

"Fine ..." She'd said wearily, "And don't worry about catching an early train tomorrow; I'll ask Tess to fill Jodie's slot until she returns. That way I won't need to *humiliate* you again."

I'd swallowed but had nodded my head, feeling more hurt than I could have possibly imagined. So; this was what it felt like to be 'washed up' at only thirty-one. I'd already pulled the door of her office open when she'd called out to me.

"Nicky?"

"Lou?"

"Tell Mike 'congratulations' ... for a job well done," she'd said drily.

I'd closed the door quietly behind me. Perhaps the trade magazine would have a vacancy for a runner ...

## Chapter Nine

The disappointment I'd felt at not seeing Aaron when I'd boarded the train at Waterloo had just about summed up my day. I hadn't even realised that the hope of seeing him had been occupying the back of my mind until the train had left the platform. Of course, he could have been anywhere on the train but some sixth sense had told me that trying to push my way through the crowded carriage in the hopes of finding him would be futile. Pity; he would have been the tonic to raise my spirits at the close of what had otherwise proved to be a crap working day. Louise had barely wished me *'goodnight'* and all I had to look forward to now was an evening with Mike.

Mike. Dear God; Louise had been right of course. I had really dug a hole for myself in agreeing to marry him but he'd taken me by surprise and with the balloons he'd arranged to adorn the table, the bouquet of twelve red roses, a box of my favourite handmade chocolates and too much wine having been consumed, when much to the amusement of some patrons, the astonishment of others and the downright disgust of still more, he'd bent down on one knee beside me, the ring nestled on its cushion inside the box as he'd held it out towards me and uttered those fateful words: *Nicky, I love you; I have always loved you. I promise, with all of my heart, that I will go on loving you and trying to make you as happy as you deserve to be until the day I die. Please, Nicky; will you give me the honour of being able to call myself your husband,* I'd been powerless to refuse; my need to end the spectacle he was making of us over-riding my common sense.

I'd watched helplessly as he'd slid the ring over my finger before he'd raised it to his lips to kiss it; almost as though he had been sealing it in place.

"A perfect fit," he'd whispered, rising a little on his knees to kiss my lips.

"It is," I'd said in a small voice, "A good guess on your part ..."

He'd chuckled, "I confess; it wasn't a guess, Angel."

"It wasn't ...?" I'd raised my eyebrows in surprise.

"No; I 'borrowed' your wedding ring and used it to have this one sized. The rest was easy ..."

"Oh ...!"

"You know; whilst a part of me is glad that you *have* kept it up until now - after all, it was certainly helpful to me in having your ring made - don't you think the time has come to get rid of it, Nicky?" he'd said, "That part of your life is over; finished. I don't even know *why* you're keeping it."

"I was keeping it for Finn ..."

He'd nodded, "I suppose I get that ... although do you really think Finn would even want it? I mean ... no offence, sweetheart but ... it's virtually worthless."

"It's sentimental I know ..."

"It's little more than a piece of tin. If you want to leave Finn something someday then leave him this ..." he'd stroked the ring now residing upon my finger and had chuckled, "If he needed it, at least this would provide him with a decent deposit on a house ..."

I'd stared at him, horrified, "Jesus, Mike! You have to be joking?"

"Of course not," he'd kissed me once more before resuming his place at the table just as Ricardo had brought over the champagne, "You're worth every last penny ... and more."

"Please don't tell me ... I don't want to know ..."

"You don't want to know that you're worth it ...?" he'd asked, a teasing smile on his lips.

"No; you know what I meant!"

"I do and I wouldn't," he'd said, "It would be most uncouth ... and it would cheapen this moment; even for me." He'd waited until Ricardo had poured the first glass of champagne and had left us alone. "To you, Nicky; my gorgeous, darling man ... and to us and our lives together," he'd raised his glass, watching as I'd followed his lead.

"To us ..." I'd murmured weakly.

"I love you, Nicky ... and there's nothing I won't do to keep you at my side."

"I love you too ..." I'd said, feeling my skin beginning to prickle.

Somehow, I couldn't help thinking that his words had been chosen with deliberate care. If alarm bells hadn't been ringing before, they'd certainly been ringing as we'd wended our way home; the last words I'd heard before I'd plugged up

## The Runner – Part 1 Nicky's Story

my ears being, *I want us to get married at the first opportunity, Nicky. We'll go down to the registry office on Monday and declare our intent to register our civil partnership; so make sure that you get the time off.*

As I'd allowed myself to recall his words, I hadn't been able to help but think that Lou had been right. The writing *was* on the wall; I just didn't want to see it. The unknown had still scared me far more.

I'd been pulled from my miserable reverie when I'd bumped shoulders with someone as I'd exited the underground station at Victoria. It had been the line of teeth, slightly out of alignment which I had recognised first. He'd looked different; not dapper but elegant, dressed as he had been in a dark pair of smart trousers, a deep red shirt with a tie to complement it which he'd worn beneath a black leather jacket. The pair of fashionable slip-on shoes he wore on his feet looked new. His hair had been neatly trimmed; his chin clean shaven and the rucksack he usually carried had been replaced with nothing more than a black umbrella. He'd seemed to be wearing something around his neck; a blue ribbon which had disappeared inside the 'V' of his fastened-up jacket. It had reminded me of the photo ID which I was required to wear around my own neck at work; a ribbon which ended with the credit card sized piece of plastic identifying me by my name, employee number as well as the name of my production company printed upon the card.

"Aaron!" I'd said breathlessly.

"Hey!" he'd smiled, "We really *must* stop meeting like this …"

## The Runner – Part 1 Nicky's Story

"Or at the very least stop knocking each other over ...!"

His smile had faded and he'd sounded apologetic, "I'm sorry I had to run out on you at lunchtime ..."

"Yeah; me too ..."

"Rush job at work," he'd said apologetically, "I ended up having a late lunch ..." His shy smile had returned, "I watched a bit of your show ..."

"Really?" I'd asked, feeling my face burn in surprise and pleasure.

He'd nodded, "You're right; you're a good salesman."

"Thanks."

"So; are you off home now?"

I'd nodded, "My train's due out in five minutes."

"Better let you go then ..."

*Oh God; I wish you wouldn't.*

"I could always get the next one ... if you fancy grabbing a coffee?" I'd ventured tentatively, "My shout this time."

"Love to ..."

"Oh, great!"

"... But I can't; if I don't get a move on, I'll be late."

"Oh!" My eyes had swept over him once more, "You've changed your outfit; you look nice ..."

## The Runner – Part 1 Nicky's Story

"Thanks ..."

"Are you going somewhere special?" I'd meant of course *are you meeting someone?*

"I guess that rather depends upon your point of view ..." I'd raised my eyebrows and he'd laughed as though he'd been able to hear my thoughts, "It's *work*; not a date ... and believe me, I'd rather be at home with a cup of coffee, adding more sugar to it than is good for me."

"Work?" I'd asked in surprise, "Jesus! How many hours do *you* work?"

"However many I'm told to," he'd said lightly, before adding, "Tonight's a one-off ..."

"Is it likely to be a late one?"

"Fairly late," he'd said and my question had seemed to be the prompt for him to glance at his watch, "Sorry, Nicky; I really have gotta run ..."

"Oh! Yes, of course; don't let me hold you up. I should run too," I'd said quickly, turning around to watch him as he'd headed towards the underground line. Only once I'd lost sight of his back had I turned in the direction of my train. I'd almost reached the barriers when I'd heard my name being called.

"Nicky!"

My breath had caught and my heart had begun to pound in my chest when I'd seen Aaron racing towards me. I'd raised my eyebrows; the gesture having been one to express both surprise and to ask the question my lips had burned to ask. *Can I see you again; properly?*

## The Runner – Part 1 Nicky's Story

He'd bitten back his smile as he'd halted three feet away from me, "I truly can't stop now and I can't do lunch tomorrow either ... but I *can* do breakfast; if you can make it?"

I'd gazed at him for a moment or two, "Are you asking me ... on a *date,* Aaron?"

"I'm inviting you to breakfast," he'd replied evenly.

I'd nodded, "Breakfast?"

"Breakfast," he'd agreed, "You *do* eat breakfast, don't you?"

"It has been known," I'd said.

"Great! So; will you meet me; tomorrow?"

"Yes," I'd heard myself saying, "Where and when?"

"Are you going to be on the same early morning service tomorrow?"

"Yes ..." *I wasn't going to be ... but I will be now!*

"I'll meet you on your train; at Clapham Junction."

"Okay; but Aaron; just to clear something up," I'd sighed as my eyes had met his, "You made your invitation sound like something else; something *more* ... well; to my ears anyway. I mean ... you *do* know that I'm gay; right?"

"Yeah; course ..." he'd laughed as he'd backed away from me, "You're Nicky Ashton; *The Living Room Mall's* current darling. Been married, now

# The Runner – Part 1 Nicky's Story

divorced; got two kids; one boy and one girl; came out three years ago ..."

My eyes had widened, "What? How ...?"

He'd shrugged, "I Googled you!"

"Why?"

"I like you," he'd said simply.

"So it *is* a date?"

"It's an 'I'd like to get to know you'," he'd replied, "Just to clear that up." He'd smiled before turning and hastening his steps, "Until tomorrow ..."

"Aaron! Wait ...!"

He'd stopped and as he'd done earlier he'd waited for me to catch him up. I'd dived into my pocket and pulled out my phone, just as the familiar announcement for my train had begun.

"Quick! Tell me your number so that I can ring your phone; then you'll have my number ... just in case something changes for either of us before morning."

He'd nodded, "Good thinking ..." And he'd rattled off his number as I'd dialled. I'd heard the muffled sound of a phone ringing and had watched as he'd pulled his iPhone out. "Okay; I've got it," he'd smiled and had nodded his head in the direction of the platform where my train was standing, "You'd better hurry."

"But ... I don't have your number!"

"I'll text you ..." I must have looked doubtful for he'd smiled to reassure me, "I promise. I have to run ... but I'll text you as soon as I get to the other end."

My train had just pulled out of Gatwick when I'd heard the text tone of my phone and had felt the vibration in my pocket. I'd opened the message and had beamed to see its length.

*I could see the questions in your eyes, so; the answers. No; I'm not playing you; yes, I'm gay; yes, I really do like you and until today, I've never hit on a guy in my life; just to clear that up! Why you? I have no idea ... but I seem to be seeing you at every turn of late. Perhaps it's fate. Just know that I'm as scared as you are. A.*

## Chapter Ten

I'd looked up from my laptop where I'd spent the best part of the evening sitting at the dining table of the open plan living area whilst I'd worked. An awareness of something in the atmosphere having changed had knocked upon the door of my unconscious mind and as a result I had begun to feel decidedly uneasy, sensing that the good mood Mike had displayed since picking me up from the station was on the verge of proving itself to be nothing more than the calm before the storm.

*Oh Jesus, Nicky. Whatever you do, don't upset him; not now.*

I'd been more than a little surprised by his cheerful demeanour as I'd hurried out of the station and into the waiting car where he'd leaned across to kiss my lips.

"Hello Angel; had a good day?"

I'd nodded, "Not bad; you?"

"Hmmm," he'd murmured, his eyes on his wing mirror, seeking a gap in the traffic. I'd watched him wave his hand in thanks at the driver who had flashed his headlights to allow us to pull out in front of him. Mike had thrown me a beaming smile, "I went to the registry office as soon as they opened this morning ..." he'd laughed, "Well, that's not quite true; I was waiting on the doorstep when the security guard unlocked the door!"

I'd felt my heart sink, "And?"

"You *did* tell Louise that you wouldn't be in on Monday, didn't you?"

# The Runner – Part 1 Nicky's Story

I'd nodded my head, "Yes."

"What did she say?"

"She wasn't very happy ..."

"But you told her?"

"I've just said so, haven't I?"

I hadn't been stupid enough not to have understood that the difference between my *asking* and *telling* Lou was the only thing that mattered to Mike. I'd never been a very good liar ... except when it came to lying to Mike. I'd become quite adept at lying then; mostly when, given the prompt, I'd told him that I loved him.

"Good ... because we have an appointment with the registrar at ten o'clock on Monday."

I'd nodded, forcing a smile for him, "Well ... that's great."

"I thought you'd be pleased ..." he'd said evenly.

"I am ..."

"Good; well this should please you even more ... we could have the ceremony as early as three weeks to the day after registering our intent."

My heart had picked up its pace at his words; not with excitement but with panic. I'd struggled to keep my tone even.

"Wow! That would be ... wonderful; but don't you think it would be a little *too* soon?"

"Would it?"

## The Runner – Part 1 Nicky's Story

"Of course it would! We can't possibly arrange a wedding in just three weeks ..."

"What's to arrange?" he'd said mildly, "It only needs you, me and two witnesses ..."

I'd laughed uncertainly. He had to be joking; didn't he?

"Are you serious, Mike?"

"Perfectly," he'd said serenely, "I thought we could take a trip to Hatton Garden this weekend and choose our wedding rings; if you'd like."

I'd felt sick. I could hardly say 'no'.

"Yeah, sure; that'd be great," I'd nodded my head, "Although ..."

"What?"

"Well ..." I'd thrown him a small smile, "I can't help feeling a little disappointed ... although perhaps that's my fault rather than yours; for imagining that you would want all the traditional trimmings for our wedding day ... and to be able to share it with our family and friends."

He'd laughed, "We have no family, Nicky; well, none that wish to acknowledge us. If they don't want to acknowledge us *now*, why would you imagine they'd feel any different once we're married? In their eyes, we'd still be living in sin; married or not."

"I was thinking of Finn and Molly," I'd said quietly, "*They* are my family; *our* family ... and I wanted them to be there."

He'd shrugged, "If Carrie will allow you to take them out of school ..."

"She wouldn't," I'd said, "And I don't want to take them out of school either. There's no need to when we can get married on a Saturday ... or even during a school holiday. I'm damned sure the Headteacher would say the same thing and for that reason, even if Carrie and I *were* prepared to remove them from school for one day, the Head wouldn't authorise such an absence."

"I've already checked, Nicky and such dates have been booked well in advance," he'd retorted, "We'd have to wait at least six months, maybe longer. And I'm not waiting that long just to fit in with the kids."

I'd sighed, "It's not *just* the kids, Mike. Don't you want our friends to be at our wedding?"

"Space is limited at the registry office, Nicky," he'd replied, "I could fill it with my friends alone ..."

I'd smiled at him, "I know ... and that's why we have to sit down and make a list of who to invite to the main event. We can invite the rest to an evening reception."

"You know all of my friends," he'd said evenly, "With the exception of Lou, I don't know any of yours ... and I'm not wasting precious seats at the registry office on people I don't even know. Therefore, in my desire to be fair to you, I've decided it would be better to invite none of them."

"What?" I'd stared at him, "Mike; don't be silly! All weddings are like that; where one side doesn't know everyone on the other. Weddings don't just unite the couple getting wed you know ..."

## The Runner – Part 1 Nicky's Story

"If we were talking about *family,* Nicky, I might agree with you," he'd said in the same even tone as before, "But we're not. I'm sorry but I'm not prepared to wine and dine a bunch of people I don't even know; *and that's an end to it.* So; far better if it's just you, me and our witnesses."

"If we waited a little while you could get to know my friends," I'd suggested.

"I've told you; I don't want to wait. I love you, Nicky and I can't wait to be married to you." He'd smiled at me and his tone had softened, "Look; we'll get married and then the four of us ... you, me and our witnesses ... can go out for a wonderful lunch; anywhere *you* choose. How's that?"

"I'll think about it," I'd replied sullenly after a long pause. It wouldn't have mattered what I'd said. In his determination to trap me, he would have had an answer ready. He always did.

"Well don't think for too long, Angel," he'd chuckled, "The registrar is a friend of mine ... and he's already pencilled us in for midday, three weeks on Monday; unofficially of course. He'll confirm the date as soon as we've registered our intent."

My eyes had widened, "You've already booked it?"

"*Unofficially,*" he'd reminded me with another chuckle.

"Don't you think you should have at least *consulted* me, Mike?"

"I did ..." he'd smiled, "I told you yesterday that I wanted us to get married at the first opportunity and you agreed. Well, as luck will have it, we can get married at midday, three weeks on Monday." He'd turned his head to glance at me, "I've already asked Les and Errol to be our witnesses and they've been more than delighted to accept."

"What?" Jesus! How much more was he going to throw at me? "But ... they're *your* friends Mike; not mine ...!"

"My friends are your friends ..."

"But mine aren't yours?"

"I can hardly count amongst my friends' people I've never met," he'd said, his tone becoming irritable, "Jesus! It's beginning to sound as if you don't *want* to get married!"

I'd bitten my lip, "Don't be silly."

"Then stop trying to put unnecessary obstacles in our way, Nicky!"

"I'm not," I'd sighed, "It's just that I had wanted to ask Lou to be my witness ..."

He'd snorted, "Even if she would agree ... which I doubt ... but even if she did, I'm not having that woman at my wedding! I've just told you that I won't wine and dine your friends when I don't know them so I'll be damned if I'll splash out on fine dining for the one friend of yours I *do* know; and one with whom the loathing is mutual between us. No; Les has agreed to act as your witness and let's face it; what does it matter, Nicky? It's a legal requirement that our signatures must be witnessed. If the law would allow me to do this my way then it would be just the two of us." He'd thrown me another smile, "So; we're agreed?"

# The Runner – Part 1 Nicky's Story

I'd nodded, unsure of how to respond to that which I knew to be a done deal. I'd been stalling; playing for the time I'd need to work up the courage to leave him. Had he known it? I didn't know. All I knew was that I had three weeks left in which to find it.

"Oh cheer up!" I'd heard him chuckle as he'd parked the car in the private car park behind our apartment block, "I picked up some brochures from the travel agents whilst I was out," he'd told me, "I thought we could have a look through them after dinner tonight and decide together where we're going to go on our honeymoon."

*You mean you'll decide and I'll agree.* "Okay ... but I've got some work to do after dinner. Perhaps once I've finished?"

Annoyance had crossed his brow in an instant but just as quickly he'd smoothed it away, "It doesn't matter. We can do it when we get back from our weekend break. There's a film on I want to watch tonight anyway."

Throughout the evening, Mike had, for once, been blissfully silent as he'd lain at full stretch on the sofa to watch his early evening film whilst I'd been going over my brief for my lunchtime show the following day. The first real flutter of panic had begun to settle in my stomach as I'd realised that his flicking through the channels had meant that the film had ended and he was becoming bored and restless at not finding anything else to watch. Words such as 'tripe' and 'crap' had begun to filter into his mutterings. No longer able to concentrate, I'd watched him, all the while hating every fibre of his being and every last hair on his head whilst his

## The Runner – Part 1 Nicky's Story

index finger had been hard at work, impatiently punching the buttons of the remote control pointed at the television set. Once or twice he'd glared at the device in his hand and had shaken it furiously before aiming it at the television again.

*"Fucking stupid thing,"* he'd hissed angrily at the device, *"Pay all that money for these things and all you get is shit ... nothing's fucking built to last these days. They do it on fucking purpose of course; just so that we poor fucking consumers have to spend even more money replacing the fuckers."* He'd shaken the device again to within an inch of its little electronic life; *"Work, will you? You fucking pile of shite!"*

I'd sighed and had risen from the table, crossing the room to the sideboard where I'd opened a drawer and removed two batteries. The last thing I'd needed was for the remote control to end up on the other side of the room; probably destroying the television screen on its way to its own demise; the first stop before mine.

"Here," I'd held the two batteries out to him, "That's all it'll be ..."

"And how the fuck would you know?" he'd snapped, snatching the batteries out of my hand and already beginning to remove the battery compartment cover from the back of the device.

I hadn't answered as I'd returned to my place at the table, my eyes fixed firmly upon the television screen. I hadn't even realised that I'd been holding my breath until I'd released it when the relief had finally flooded through my veins as the channels had begun to change without pause. Resisting the

## The Runner – Part 1 Nicky's Story

yearning to utter the words 'I told you so', I'd returned my attention to my laptop. I'd closed my eyes and bitten down on my lip when the room had suddenly been plunged into silence.

"How much bloody longer are you going to be, Nicky?" Mike had demanded sharply, tossing the remote control onto the coffee table, "You've been sat at that table all fucking night."

"Not long ..." I'd answered quietly, "Half an hour; maybe an hour."

"An hour?" he'd sat up, swinging his legs over the side of the sofa, glaring at me all the while, "Do you actually *do* any work whilst you're at that place; or do you have to bring it home with you because you spend your whole day tucked up in Louise's office, drinking coffee whilst you both slag me off?"

"We don't slag you off ..."

"Ah! So you *do* talk about me?"

"We talk about work ... and I don't spend all day in her office."

"Not much ..."

"Why are you having a go at me?" I'd asked. He'd been spoiling for a fight I hadn't wanted to give him, "I did tell you that I had some work to do ... and you've been watching a film!"

"Yeah, well; it's finished now ..."

I'd sighed, "I won't be long, Mike; I promise."

"What the hell are you doing anyway?"

"I have a guest on tomorrow's show; the managing director of a small company we've never

## The Runner – Part 1 Nicky's Story

used before. I've never met her and she's never appeared on television before. I was only shown the products we'll be featuring late this afternoon and I want to be well prepared; make sure it all goes smoothly. I need to know what I'm talking about; especially if my guest should turn out to be a bit camera shy; as some of them are ..."

"I don't care who you've got on your bloody show tomorrow ..." he'd got up and had come to stand over me, slamming closed my laptop as he'd leaned towards me, "Enough Nicky; I want to go to bed."

I'd felt my heart begin to pound in my chest, "I'm not stopping you ..." I'd said serenely as I'd opened my laptop up again.

He'd slammed it shut for the second time, "Do that again and you won't *have* a laptop," he'd warned me, "You're not listening to me, Nicky. I said; *I want to go to bed.*" He'd enunciated each word slowly and deliberately so that I would not mistake his meaning.

Of course, I could have refused; I *should* have refused; but I didn't. The fire I had found in my soul just two days ago when I'd spent the night locked securely behind the door of the spare bedroom had gone out and I'd had no idea of how to ignite it again. Perhaps too I'd perceived the ring on my finger to have been the final proof of ownership ...

I'd nodded and had got up from the table, throwing him a contrite smile. "I'm sorry; you're right. I shouldn't be doing this now ..."

# The Runner – Part 1 Nicky's Story

**oOo**

Wrapped in my dressing gown and with a cup of coffee in my hand, I'd curled up in my armchair and had switched on the television set, taking care to turn the volume down to prevent the sound from carrying across the hall to the bedroom where I'd left Mike snoring.

A quick skim through the on-screen programme guide had led me to an early-hours-of-the-morning broadcast of the recording of a live transmission only a few hours earlier. A glance at the synopsis had me pressing the button to select to view a programme that Mike's impatience would never have allowed me to watch even if I had known it had been on. Watching a bunch of film stars arrive for a red carpet premiere wasn't necessarily my idea of fun either but in this instance it featured my favourite actor; one who had unwittingly provided me with more than a few pleasurable moments alone in the shower.

As the main attraction, he would be one of the last to arrive and so I'd listened to the interviews of the supporting cast members whilst along with the crowds waiting outside of the cinema in Leicester Square, I had eagerly awaited the arrival of the young star. God! What I wouldn't have given to have been able to have had a ticket for *that* particular cinema tonight!

I'd known from the screaming of the crowd that the actor had arrived and barely had his face appeared on the screen when I'd set my cup down on the coffee table whilst my free hand had stolen

154

# The Runner – Part 1 Nicky's Story

beneath my dressing gown to seek out the pleasure I had longed for but could no longer find from Mike. Yes; the writing had most assuredly been on the wall and despite all that Lou had said to the contrary I could see it only too clearly. My problem lay in not knowing how to respond.

I had been gently drifting towards the moment where I would lose myself to nothing more than the sound of the actor's voice when my eyes had strayed to the screen. It hadn't registered at first and I'd closed my eyes, allowing my hand to work a little faster, eliciting the first, deep groan of pleasure. Suddenly, the image I'd seen had filtered into my brain and my hand had halted abruptly. It couldn't be! Ignoring the almost painful throbbing in my groin which had been demanding my urgent attention, I'd sat up and leaned towards the screen which had still been filled with the smiling face of the object of my lust. It was no longer him I had been interested in however; someone else had caught my eye.

"Oh ... my ... God! I don't believe it! You jammy bastard ...!"

My eyes had almost popped out of my head and my pulse had begun to race even faster than it had been up to that moment. There, just in view of the camera and standing not too far from my actor, was Aaron. I'd almost laughed out loud. He couldn't have looked any more bored if he'd tried and the expression upon his face had made it perfectly clear to me that he was finding the whole event exceedingly tedious. In an instant, I had understood the purpose of the blue ribbon around his neck; it had been his security pass for this event. Bastard! I could have scratched his eyes out in my envy of him being so close to the guilty pleasure of my dreams ... and there *he* was leaving me in no doubt that he hadn't been joking about his preference for a cup of coffee with more sugar than was good for him!

What the hell was *Aaron* doing at such an event? He'd said he was working tonight so what was it that he did exactly? He didn't appear to be security and since he didn't have a microphone in his hand, I didn't have the impression that he was there to interview these stars of the silver screen. I'd shaken my head in frustration, desperate to know why he was there.

The actor had moved on a few steps and I'd thought I'd been thrown a small crumb of a clue when I'd clearly seen the word PRESS printed upon Aaron's security pass. My eyes had widened; was that what he did? Was he a celebrity journalist of some sort? Perhaps; although if he was, it didn't look to me as though he was going to have much to write about since he'd been making no effort with any of these big names. Still; hadn't he said that his degree was in Television and Media? Not that I'd really known exactly what such a description truly meant. Nonetheless, to me, PRESS and Media were words which fitted together in the same way that Jack went with Jill, Tarzan belonged with Jane and ... Nicky blended with Aaron.

I'd hurried to the guest bathroom and when relief had finally found me, it was Aaron's face in my mind's eye and his name which had rushed past my lips.

## Chapter Eleven

It had been hard to know which emotion had been the stronger as I'd boarded the early train the following morning. Fear that within a couple of hours, Mike would find out that Lou had dropped me from Jodie's show or elation that in him not having questioned me last evening, I had successfully deceived him this morning; despite the hell it would cost me later. Somehow, Aaron had already seemed to be worth the risk and my heart had leapt for joy when the train had pulled out of my home station to carry me towards my illicit tryst.

My heart had lurched momentarily when I'd heard the text tone of my phone. Shit! Had Mike somehow found out already? No; he couldn't have done. It was too early for him to have rung Lou and besides, what reason would he have had for doing so? The only thing that I'd had any confidence in was the certain knowledge that Lou would never have called my home number even if *she* had had reason to call me.

I'd glanced at the message icon on the screen and had opened it to be greeted with a number rather than a name. Aware that Mike policed my call and message logs, I had deliberately not added Aaron's name to my 'contacts' directory, since convincing Mike that an unknown number must have called mine in error would be a damned sight simpler than trying to have to explain another man's name in my phone.

"Hey! Good morning! Where are you?" I'd read.

## The Runner – Part 1 Nicky's Story

I'd smiled to myself as I'd tapped out my reply, *"Train's just left East Croydon; will see you in a few minutes."*

*"Great! When I hadn't heard from you, I'd wondered if perhaps you'd changed your mind."*

*"I didn't want to seem ... pushy. I haven't changed my mind; and I'm glad that you haven't either."* I'd stared at the screen for a few seconds, debating the word in my mind; should I replace *glad* with *happy*? I'd used the backspace key to replace the word. It was perfectly acceptable for me to be happy to be seeing him; wasn't it? Or did it sound pushier than simply being glad? *For Heaven's sake, Nicky; just send it! He's waiting for you so I'm sure he won't care which you choose!* I'd settled for *happy* and had pressed send.

*"Can see your train ... which carriage?"*

*"Three ..."*

*"Thanks; am lined up for six or seven ...!"*

*"Better run then ...!"*

*"x."*

I'd stared at the screen, inwardly hugging myself to see the representation for a kiss. My smile had broadened when the train had stopped and only moments later I'd heard his soft voice as he'd dropped into the seat opposite me.

*"The first thing you need to know about me, Nicky, is that I never run anywhere!"*

I'd laughed as my eyes had met his, *"What's the second?"*

He'd smiled and his eyes had been twinkling at me, "My idea of breakfast generally centres round a certain fast food chain. What's yours?"

"Strong coffee; several," I'd replied.

He'd raised his eyebrows, "Really; is that it?"

"I'm a cheap date," I'd quipped lightly.

"I doubt you're cheap," he'd said, "And it's not a date ..."

"Ah! No. It's a 'getting to know you' ..."

"It is," he'd agreed, "And already we've learned that we have *two* things in common."

"Two?" I'd raised my eyebrows.

He'd nodded, "We share an interest in our work ... and neither of us has a healthy start to our day. *Your* unhealthy habits continue to the lunch hour of course ..."

I'd laughed, "Ah yes! The four shots ..."

"Do you *really* do that?"

I'd shaken my head, "No. I just get too involved in the novels I read ..."

"Care to explain?" he'd asked as the train had pulled into the platform at Victoria.

I'd gathered up my laptop bag and had folded my coat over my arm, "I'll tell you on the way to the burger joint."

We'd left the station and had ambled along the still fairly quiet street, falling into conversation as easily as we had the previous day. After persuading

## The Runner – Part 1 Nicky's Story

me towards a breakfast meal, Aaron had once again waved away any efforts on my part to pay.

"I invited *you*, remember?"

"I know but I was expecting this one to be my shout."

He'd merely smiled and had carried our tray to a table in a quiet corner. "It'll get busy soon," he'd said, "At least here we should be able to talk with some degree of privacy."

I'd nodded and had sat down opposite him. "So," I'd begun with a smile, "At the moment I would say the 'getting to know you' is stacked firmly in your favour. I'd like to know more about you."

"What would you like to know?" he'd asked, adding sugar to his coffee.

"Well," I'd said slowly, "I have to admit I'm rather curious as to why I saw you on TV in the early hours of this morning."

He'd raised his eyebrows, looking confused, "On TV?"

"Hmmm; I saw you on the red carpet in Leicester Square."

"The cameras caught *me*?" he'd asked in surprise whilst a feint pink hue had risen to colour his cheeks.

"They certainly did!" I'd told him.

"Oh shit …!"

"What the hell is it you do for a living, Aaron that would have you standing within touching distance of the most gorgeous man on the planet …

# The Runner – Part 1 Nicky's Story

*and* might I add looking bored to death; as though you'd rather be at home with of a cup of cocoa!"

He'd laughed, "I would have ..."

"Are you a reporter; or perhaps you're in security?"

"Neither," he'd said, biting into his egg and bacon muffin. The grease from the contents sandwiched between the bread had begun to slide down his chin into the overnight stubble and he'd snatched up a paper napkin to mop it up, "God; I'm sorry. How uncouth ...!"

I'd smiled, hardly liking to tell him that I'd have liked to mop it up for him; with my tongue. "Don't apologise ... it's kind of *cute*."

"Whatever floats your boat ..." he'd shrugged but he'd thrown me a coy smile just the same.

"So come on; tell me why you were on the red carpet last night ... with him!"

"Who are we talking about?" he'd asked innocently and I'd known that he'd been teasing me; that he'd known exactly to whom I'd been referring.

"Aaron!"

He'd laughed, "Firstly, I wasn't *with him* ... and secondly, my reason for being there doesn't have quite the glamour you seem to think!" He'd paused to sip his coffee. "My company was engaged to go along to do a little filming of the event; for one of the TV networks."

"Wow!"

"My brief was to wait for the first lot of rushes and get them back to my office where our editors

## The Runner – Part 1 Nicky's Story

were anxiously waiting for them," he'd smiled at me, "Once they'd done *their* job, I had to run them over to the network who had commissioned us for the filming." He'd taken another sip of coffee, "That's what I do; I'm a runner."

"Ah!" I'd smiled as I'd understood. "Would I be right in thinking that your job involves a lot of travelling around the underground to various studios?"

He'd nodded, "I can be sent anywhere at any time; and most of the time I'm on a tight deadline," he'd thrown me an amused smile, "I certainly couldn't ever afford to get on the wrong train as you did the other day!"

I'd laughed, "I'd hoped that you hadn't realised."

"And I'd hoped that you *had* done it on purpose ..."

"It was more of a 'distracted accident' ..." I'd said with a sheepish smile, "Although if you'd hoped it was deliberate, it has to be said that you didn't exactly give me any encouragement to try to engage with you. You plugged into your iPod!"

He'd shrugged, "I felt out of my depth ... and it's not as though we were in a nightclub with the booze flowing."

"Yeah; I get that. I admit that I felt the same ... although I had been ready to make the effort." I'd smiled at him, "If you had given me the slightest sign that you might be willing to talk to me, I was even prepared to miss my stop; but you didn't ..."

"Sorry ..."

## The Runner – Part 1 Nicky's Story

"So; how long have you been a runner?" I'd asked into the short silence which had seemed to momentarily fall between us.

He'd shrugged, "About six months. It's not the job I applied for or wanted but although I have the knowledge, being only a year out of Uni, I lacked the experience. When the MD rang to offer me this position as an alternative, I considered myself lucky. Many of my friends are still trying to find an opening in the industry; anywhere. I thought this position might have potential; later on."

I'd smiled at him, "So until then, you spend your life on underground trains ..."

"That just about sums it up," he'd agreed, smiling at me, "I told you that it wasn't glamorous!"

"You enjoy it though?"

"It pays the bills ... and as I've said; it might lead to other things."

"I imagine you must know your way around the underground pretty well?"

"Yep!" he'd said lightly, smiling at me, "So well in fact that as a side-line, I'm in the process of compiling a travel guide. You know the kind of thing; *The London Underground for Dummies* ..."

"Are you?" I'd asked, suitably impressed.

He'd rolled his eyes and had chuckled, "No!"

I'd felt my cheeks warming as I'd realised he'd been poking fun at his job. "I bet you could though ..."

"Probably," he'd agreed, his eyes gleaming in amusement, "But I don't think I will. Writing isn't

## The Runner – Part 1 Nicky's Story

for me ... as I found out when it came to writing my dissertation for my degree. I think I'll reserve my knowledge as a party trick or for pub quizzes perhaps. Course, it could prove useful if I lose my job and need to apply for a position washing platforms ..."

I'd laughed. "Do you live in London?" I'd asked him.

He'd nodded, "Not too far from Clapham Junction."

"Do you still live with your parents?"

"No; I live in a shared house with three others. It's nothing special but it's reasonably cheap, comfortable and ideally situated for me getting in and out of Central London," he'd smiled, "It's not very much different from sharing with students; just a lot cleaner and tidier!"

I'd smiled, "So where's 'home'? From your accent I'd thought the North somewhere; I thought I'd detected the smallest North East twang."

"I'm from the South East originally but I lived just outside of Durham for seven years. We moved back just before I began my 'A' Levels. Mum couldn't settle after my Dad died, so her brother persuaded her to move back with me and my younger brother."

"Do you have a good relationship with your family?"

"We're all very close," he'd agreed.

"Do they know that you're gay?"

"They know," he'd smiled, "Not that I've ever told them but there's no need for me to. They know and I know that they know and it's fine."

"You're very lucky."

"Yes," he'd agreed, "I know."

"Where do your Mum and brother live?"

"Eastbourne ..."

I'd heard my sharp intake of breath, "You're kidding?"

He'd raised his eyebrows, "No; why?"

"I don't live too far from Eastbourne! My God! Talk about coincidence. It's almost beginning to seem like ..." I'd come to an abrupt halt and had looked away, feeling my face burning.

"Fate?" he'd supplied.

"It just seems weird, that's all. I've been bumping into you all week; seeing you at almost every turn - as you pointed out yesterday - and now you tell me that your family live quite near to me. It's so ... surreal."

He'd smiled, "Believe me, Nicky; you don't have to explain it to me. I'm part of this ... *thing;* whatever it is and so I know *exactly* what you mean and how you're feeling."

"I even saw you in the book shop the other day ..." I'd told him.

"I saw you too."

"Did you?" I'd asked, surprised, "I hadn't realised."

### The Runner – Part 1 Nicky's Story

"You were with someone; an older woman."

"Lou," I'd nodded, smiling to myself whilst I'd considered how irked Lou would have been to hear any description of her containing the word 'old'. 'Mature' would have sat better with her. "She's my Executive Producer ... and a very dear friend; well, she's more like a mother to me really."

"Yeah; I kind of got that impression." He'd looked embarrassed as he'd rushed on to explain, "You didn't see me but ... I followed you both to the coffee shop."

I'd raised my eyebrows, "You *followed* us?"

"It's crazy," he'd said, shaking his head, "I didn't intend to; it just sort of ... happened; probably in much the same way as it did for you when you followed me onto the Northern line." He'd nodded and had laughed to see me blush, "I recognised the confusion on your face. It was quite funny really. I'd felt exactly the same way when I'd found myself standing at the counter of the coffee shop. I couldn't even remember how I'd got there! When I turned around to leave, I suddenly spotted you and your friend sitting at a table and so I ordered a coffee and sat down behind you."

My eyes had widened in surprise, "I didn't see you!"

"No, I know," he'd said quietly. "Nicky; I have a confession to make ..."

"Oh?"

"I overheard your conversation," he'd suddenly looked sheepish, "No I didn't; that's a lie. I *listened* to your conversation."

## The Runner – Part 1 Nicky's Story

"You *listened*?"

He'd nodded, "I heard everything; in fact I stayed to listen. I'm sorry."

"You heard ... *everything*?"

"Yes," he'd agreed mildly, "Every last word that passed between you."

*Shit! That means he knows about Mike.* "Oh my God ...!"

He'd bitten his lip, "I noticed you for the first time about three months ago and for the past few weeks at least, I've been trying to figure out a way to make you notice *me* ... but I'm crap at that sort of thing. I've always been rather ... *reserved* and I'm rubbish with perfect strangers. I'd just about given up on the idea when suddenly, this week, not only did you seem to have finally noticed me but we kept bumping into each other; quite literally ... and still I hadn't a clue as to how to approach you; let alone know if I should!"

I'd laughed, "I know the feeling ..."

He'd nodded, "I'd started to see it as a sign; began to truly believe that it was fated for you and me to meet ... and just as I thought it was going to happen; well, as I've said; I heard all that passed between you and your friend." His eyes had met mine, "I Googled you out of curiosity but it was in the coffee shop where I learned that you're gay; from your conversation with your friend. I mean, I kind of knew that you *were* but ... well; it was just nice to *know;* before I made a complete fool of myself." He'd paused and had released a heavy sigh, "It's also on account of all that I heard that this

## The Runner – Part 1 Nicky's Story

isn't a 'date'. I'd have liked it to have been but ... well; Fate hadn't allowed me to consider that you might have a boyfriend ... and I don't do affairs."

I'd gazed at Aaron steadily. He wouldn't have known it of course but affairs were not my forte either. Perhaps – technically speaking - Mike *had* been an affair since I'd still been married to Carrie when I'd met him but I hadn't viewed it that way. I'd seen it as my true self struggling to surface; begging me to allow it to breathe; to be heard. Mike had been the beginning of my journey; teaching me to be able to acknowledge who I was; to publicly embrace it. He'd been the path to me finding my courage, regardless that it was going to hurt so many; including me. But was my journey destined to end with him?

I'd bitten my lip as Lou's words of a few days ago had crept back into my mind. Perhaps she had been right in some ways. I'd moved from one closet to another; one which had felt safe ... at the time. Mike had been a crutch of sorts; one I'd no longer needed and most assuredly didn't want and he for his part had liked me because my fears had made me easy to control and if there was one thing Mike liked and needed above all else, it was to be in control; of everything and everyone around him; rather like his company before he'd sold it.

In that moment, it was as though a switch had been flicked in my brain and I'd understood why my life had become so unbearable since Mike had taken early retirement. I'd become *his* crutch; for his loneliness and to fill his need to be 'in charge' of everything; and he'd resented the hell out of me because he'd needed me. Suddenly I'd realised that

## The Runner – Part 1 Nicky's Story

I had been stronger than I'd thought. I'd had to be if Mike had believed it and clearly he had. Why else would he have wished to feed my fears; crush my spirit? And hadn't he told me only two days ago that he would do anything to keep me at his side?

I'd shivered involuntarily as I'd realised that our relationship had run its course long before he'd sold the company ... and I'd known that there must have come a point when Mike had sensed it too. We'd become a comfortable bad habit but Mike had feared being alone even more than I had and he'd rather have had me broken than not to have had me at all. He'd sold the company in order to keep me within his sights; to be around me every single moment that I wasn't working; to ensure that I hadn't had space to breathe; to *think* ... and he'd used his time with me wisely; making me afraid to stay but even more afraid to leave.

Aware that Aaron had still been watching me, I'd sighed and had thrown him a weak smile.

"I don't do affairs either," I'd said, "And yet you're here and I'm here. *We're* here."

He'd returned my weak smile with one of his own, "We're here, Nicky through impulse on my part and unhappiness on yours. I've carried around this inexplicable gut feeling for weeks now and even though I know it to be ridiculous ..." He'd shaken his head, "Perhaps we're here simply because I want to be able to put these idiotic feelings to bed once and for all."

"I'm not sure that I understand?" I'd said uncertainly, the hopes I'd brought to our breakfast soiree suddenly beginning to disintegrate. It had

## The Runner – Part 1 Nicky's Story

begun to sound as though he wasn't as interested in me as I'd thought. But then; *I* hadn't known that *he'd* known about Mike.

He'd sighed, "For me, it feels as though everything has been leading to this one moment; as if it will define something for me. Even the stupid things I've done of late ... well; they defy explanation."

"What things?"

He'd shrugged, "Following you and your friend to a coffee shop, making a concerted effort to be on the same mainline service as you each evening when there are so many others I can catch to Clapham Junction; running after you yesterday; twice ..."

"Twice?"

He'd laughed, "You think that my being in the coffee shop at lunchtime was a coincidence?"

"It wasn't?"

He'd rolled his eyes, "No! Of course it wasn't. I almost *threw* my package over the reception desk just to be able to run out again in the hopes of catching you up!"

"Did you bump into me on purpose too; before you went into my building?"

"No," he'd shaken his head, "The credit for that small incident belongs firmly to our little friend, Fate ... and the network who suddenly decided that they wished to promote last night's premiered film on their lunchtime magazine programme." He'd smiled, "However; my being at Victoria last night was no more of a coincidence than lunch yesterday. After I received that call at lunchtime, I went straight home to change and then returned to my office in Westminster. It was from there that I set out for Leicester Square. To get there via Victoria meant changing trains twice. It would have been quicker and easier for me to get on the Northern line from Embankment ... not least because I would only have had to change trains once."

"You *orchestrated* our meeting last night?"

"Only in the sense that I'd been counting on you to catch your usual train," he'd confessed, "And do you know what? I still don't really know why I did."

"You don't usually go to such lengths to meet guys then?" I'd asked lightly.

He'd laughed, "I might be a runner ... but believe me; I *never* do the running. Being so bold as to ask you to meet me this morning is so far out of character for me that none of my friends would recognise me. Hell; I don't even recognise myself!"

"Yet you did run after me ..." I'd said with a small smile, "I'd be flattered ... if I wasn't beginning to get the sense that this is turning into a 'see you around' rather than a 'getting to know you' meeting."

He'd smiled, "Perhaps I *needed* to meet you ... in order to be able to forget you; stop thinking about you and wondering what might be if we could only meet. As I've already said; put to bed once and for all these weird feelings I have for and about you."

### The Runner – Part 1 Nicky's Story

"And have you? Put the feelings to bed?"

"No," he'd shaken his head and had sighed, "I think I've made it harder for myself to be able to do that." His eyes had met mine, "I *really* like you, Nicky and talking to you yesterday and now; well, I don't even know you and yet I feel as though I've known you forever." He'd laughed, "It's weird ... and it's scaring me to death."

I'd hardly known what to say as we'd sat facing each other. It seemed he had finally run out of words and I for my part, hadn't been able to find any.

"Do you believe in Fate?" he'd asked me suddenly, "Or even Destiny?"

Had he been asking me if I'd believed that he was my destiny and I, his? Despite the fact that we'd only just met, I'd found myself to be hoping that it was exactly what he had been asking.

"I never used to ..." I'd said evenly, "Fate; Destiny; love at first sight; I'd always thought that only a fool would believe in such things."

"And now?"

"I'm a fool!"

He'd smiled, "Me too."

I'd nodded my head slowly at him as we'd watched each other across the table. When I'd stood up, he'd raised his eyebrows.

"Are you leaving?"

"Do you want me to?" I'd asked.

"No," he'd shaken his head.

## The Runner – Part 1 Nicky's Story

"Then fine; I was going to offer you another coffee."

He'd chuckled, "They don't serve brandy, do they?"

"I don't think so, no," I'd smiled at him.

"Shucks! I think I could have put one to good use."

"You wouldn't drink at this hour would you?"

"Hey! I'm an ex-student; what do you think?"

"I think I'm suddenly worried for your liver ..."

"Well don't! It's been slowly and lovingly pickled over the past four years, so it's been well preserved. It'll last a while yet ..."

"Please tell me you're joking."

"I'm joking; fetch the coffee."

## **Chapter Twelve**

Aaron had smiled as I'd set the insulated paper cup down on the table in front of him.

"Thanks."

"You're welcome ... although I do wish you'd let me pay for breakfast."

"Another time perhaps ..."

I'd raised my eyebrows, "Do you want there to be 'another time'?"

"That rather depends ..."

"Upon ...?"

"What happens in the next half an hour or so I guess; that is providing you haven't got to rush off yet."

I'd shaken my head, surprising myself in my sudden resolution to call Lou before breakfast was over, "I haven't got anywhere to rush off to; not today."

"Day off?"

"Not exactly," I'd said, removing the plastic lid from my cup and blowing on the liquid in my efforts to cool it. I'd told him the truth, adding a little embroidery to the fabric, "I've been taken off-air; for the show I was covering ... as well as my own."

He'd raised his eyebrows, "You've been taken off-air; for your own show ... why?"

"A disagreement with Lou ... she's very upset with me; angry even. Taking me off-air is something

# The Runner – Part 1 Nicky's Story

of a cooling off period; for both of us; before either of us says something we'll regret."

"You make it sound as though the disagreement was personal. Would it be too rude of me to ask what it was about?"

"Sure; why not?" I'd shrugged, "I rather think it's going to become relevant to our conversation."

"Well?"

"If you really did hear every word of my conversation with Lou then you'll already know that she can't stand my boyfriend, Mike," I'd begun, "Two nights ago ... the very night of the day I was in the coffee shop with Lou ... he asked me to marry him; and I accepted."

"Oh; I see," he'd said, his tone flat.

"No you don't," I'd shaken my head, "Lou's upset because she knows I've got myself into a right mess; purely because I'm a coward. And now that I'm in it, I'm not sure how I'm going to get myself out of it."

"What do you mean?"

"I don't love Mike; not any longer ..." I'd sighed, "I haven't loved him for a very long time and he certainly doesn't love me."

Aaron had frowned, "If he doesn't love you then why would he have asked you to marry him?"

I'd bitten my lip, the truth of my words hitting me as I'd spoken, "Mike's a businessman; or was. He owned a very successful scaffolding company until he sold it a little over a year ago. I'm a commodity; one he's decided he needs in order to

# The Runner – Part 1 Nicky's Story

combat having to be alone. At fifty-three, I don't think he fancies the idea of having to start over again with someone else. He runs our lives ... runs *me* in much the same way as he ran his business. He still needs *something* to control."

"And that something is you?"

"I don't have an easy ride with him ..." I'd said quietly; ashamed and embarrassed to be admitting to such cowardice.

"Then ... why *on Earth* would you have agreed to marry him, Nicky?" Aaron had asked in a tone of disbelief, "If you *know* all this about him; you; your relationship?"

I'd smiled, "It must all seem so very simple to you – the notion of turning him down, I mean. It does to me; when I'm sitting here and he's miles away ... but I live with him, Aaron and when you're faced with someone like Mike every day, if you're not stronger than he is, well; it's a completely different story. In his presence, I just seem to freeze. I seem to have lost the ability to stand up for myself."

"You're afraid of him ...?"

I'd bitten my lip, "I didn't think I was but ..." I'd nodded, "the simple truth is yes; I suppose I am. He's so volatile that it scares me to death to be perfectly frank. I feel as though I'm walking on eggshells at home most of the time. I'm constantly trying to gauge his mood and adjust my own behaviour accordingly; and even if I assess his mood correctly, it can change quicker than the wind can change direction."

"Is he violent towards you?"

"Not exactly, no. Generally he restricts himself to yelling and throwing things at me," I'd smiled weakly, "Usually it's the TV remote."

"Generally; but not always?"

I'd blushed, "Let's just say that the bedroom is the place where he's most likely to be less than loving. It hasn't been a happy experience for me for a long while."

Aaron too had blushed to his roots, "I'm sorry."

I'd smiled at him, "That's usually my line. It seems to be my best defence; providing my behaviour supports my contrition."

"Why don't you just leave him?"

I'd laughed, "I ask myself that very question at least a hundred times a day! I'm hoping that one day I might be able to answer it." I'd sighed, "Although I'm almost out of time now; to find the answer."

"What do you mean?"

"Mike told me last night that we're getting married in a little over three weeks."

His eyes had widened, "He *told* you?"

I'd smiled, "I must cut quite a pathetic figure to you."

"No," he'd shaken his head, "I just don't understand why you would allow a man to control you as you seem to be suggesting that Mike controls you ... but then again I've never been afraid."

## The Runner – Part 1 Nicky's Story

"Never?" I'd raised my eyebrows.

"Only when I was awaiting my exam results …" He'd sighed, "So what are you going to do, Nicky?"

I'd bitten my lip as the first tears had fallen. "I don't know …" I'd whispered.

Aaron had reached across the table to wipe away some of the tears with his thumb, "Oh, hey! Don't cry …" he'd pleaded softly, "I didn't mean to upset you …"

"You haven't …"

He'd glanced around him, "It's getting busy; let's get out of here."

"I'm embarrassing you …"

"No you're not," he'd smiled, "I'm thinking of your street cred …"

"What?"

"Just because *I* didn't know who you are doesn't mean that I'm in the majority …" he'd replaced the plastic lid on my coffee cup and had stood up. "Come on," he'd held the cup and his hand out to me, "Let's go somewhere else; somewhere quiet."

I'd looked up at him, "Quiet; in London?"

"I know of somewhere …"

"Where?"

"Somewhere near Clapham Junction …"

My eyes had widened, "Are you inviting me to your place?"

# The Runner – Part 1 Nicky's Story

"Unless you can think of somewhere better ...?" I'd shaken my head and he'd smiled, "I'm guessing you have a season ticket for the train?"

I'd nodded, "Yes."

"Well? Do you want to use it?"

I'd hesitated, suddenly feeling more out of my depth then I did with Mike, "Do *you* want me to?"

He'd shaken his head, "No, Nicky; that decision is yours. I'm not Mike ... I won't make it for you."

**oOo**

"Make yourself at home whilst I put the kettle on." Aaron had peeled off his jacket and had draped it over the arm of the sofa; something I would never have dared to do at home. "I'm presuming that a coffee addict such as you seem to be, *would* like a coffee?"

I'd nodded, "Yes please."

"It's instant ... so an extra shot will be an extra teaspoonful; if you want it," he'd said evenly, though his lips had been twitching.

"However you make it will be fine," I'd said, "And don't take the piss ..."

He'd laughed, "Take your coat off, Nicky ... I promise I don't bite."

"I didn't think you did," I'd smiled at him, "Where should I hang it?"

"Lay it over the top of mine for now ..."

## The Runner – Part 1 Nicky's Story

"This isn't a bad place," I'd said, taking in my surroundings whilst shrugging out of my coat.

He'd grinned at me from the doorway to the hall, "You sound surprised."

"I am to be perfectly honest with you," I'd admitted, feeling a little embarrassed, "It's better than I'd been expecting."

He'd laughed, "It doesn't look much from the outside, does it?"

"No," I'd smiled, "I guess it proves that one shouldn't judge a book by its cover. I had you down as a layabout student …"

"Thanks …"

"Sorry …" I'd pulled an apologetic face whilst continuing to look around the room; taking in the few pictures hanging on the walls. A large photograph frame on the mantle above the fireplace had caught my eye and since it hadn't contained a photograph, I'd taken a few steps towards it to take a closer look. Confusion had crossed my brow when I'd realised that the frame contained a cheque and a payslip; both with Aaron's name typed upon them; *Mr Aaron J Walker.*

I'd turned to where he'd still been standing in the doorway watching me. "What does the 'J' stand for?"

"Joseph …"

"Your second Christian name is Joseph? So is mine …"

He'd grinned at me, "I know; your full name came up in my Google search of you. Another

## The Runner – Part 1 Nicky's Story

coincidence ... and three things we have in common!"

"God! That's almost freaky! We don't share a birthday do we?"

"No; my birthday is in July," he'd laughed, "But our star signs work; totally compatible in fact. I've checked!"

I too had laughed, "You've been busy ..."

"I've told you; I like you ... perhaps more than will prove to be good for me."

I'd raised my eyebrows, trying to ignore the butterflies desperate to escape the cage of my stomach. I'd pointed to the frame on the mantelpiece and had changed the subject. "You've worked for the BBC?"

He'd shrugged, "It was whilst I was in my second year at Uni. The programme makers approached the professor of my degree course and asked if a few of his undergraduate students would like to take part for a couple of days ... and get paid for it. A few of us were available so ... we did."

"Oh really?" I'd raised my eyebrows, "What did you do for them?"

Aaron had laughed, "If you're thinking that it was something glamorous, it wasn't. It was no more glamorous than my job now. Basically we sat in a bloody hard plastic chair for two days ... each of us with a carrier bag at our feet stuffed full of nothing more than newspaper!"

"What?"

## The Runner – Part 1 Nicky's Story

"It was for an antiques programme. We had front row seats where our brief was to pretend to be members of the public waiting to have our antiques valued by the experts!"

I'd raised my eyebrows, "You were … *plants?*"

"That's one way of looking at it I suppose."

"Do they really do that; fake it?"

"When the crowds are thinning …"

"Wow! What a con …!" I'd said.

He'd laughed, "Oh come on, Nicky; its television! A set; a stage … you know how it is."

"I'd always thought it was utterly real …" I'd said, "And now you're telling me that some of those people have nothing more than screwed up *newspaper* in their bags …"

"And just as many don't," he'd shrugged, "The rest is just an illusion. It's not hurting anyone and who really cares? Not the viewing public … as long as what they're watching provides them with an hour of decent entertainment, they're perfectly happy."

"You really got paid for sitting with a carrier bag full of newspaper at your feet?" I'd asked incredulously.

"Yep; I really did." He'd chuckled, "Although trust me; whilst sitting in a chair for two bloody days solid might sound like easy money, it isn't. By the end of it, my arse and my back ached so much that at sixty quid for two days' work, I felt like a cheap trick!"

"Yet you never cashed the cheque?"

# The Runner – Part 1 Nicky's Story

"No," he'd laughed, "My Mum gave me the sixty quid and told me to keep the cheque; as a souvenir of sorts!"

"The payslip wasn't souvenir enough?"

"You don't know my Mum. You can't have Adam without Eve ..."

I'd felt myself smiling, "Did she frame them for you?"

"No," he'd shaken his head, "My friend Kevin did that; as a joke; just after we moved here."

"You moved here *with your friend?*" I'd asked, surprised to hear the wavering note of jealousy in my tone, "Is Kevin gay?"

"Yes, he is; why?"

"Is he a *close* friend?"

"He's just a friend, Nicky," he'd said evenly, "I've already told you I don't do affairs; and if I did, I can assure you that I wouldn't be stupid enough to shit on my own doorstep. I don't do fuck buddies either; just to clear that up too."

"Sorry; it's none of my business ..." I'd murmured, suddenly feeling embarrassed and exceedingly stupid. Aaron wasn't mine and therefore I had no right to question him over his private life.

He'd sighed, "I'm not the one with a 'complication' in my life, Nicky; should you and I discover that we have anything to even consider. Kevin and I were at Uni together and we came to London together; end of. Okay?"

I'd nodded, "Okay. I'm sorry ..."

## The Runner – Part 1 Nicky's Story

"You don't need to apologise," he'd said lightly, "And I guess I don't blame you for asking; in the circumstances."

"In the circumstances ...?"

"Well; this *is* supposed to be a 'getting to know you' ..." He'd smiled, "I won't be long. Nicky, please sit down; you're making the place look like a student house."

"Huh?"

"Untidy ..." he'd grinned at me and had disappeared.

From my place perched on the edge of the sofa, I could hear him in the kitchen which from the noises coming from it, had sounded as though it might be at the end of the hall. I'd heard him flick the switch on the kettle; heard a cupboard door open, followed by the clink of crockery. A drawer opened and I'd heard him rifling through the cutlery, presumably looking for a teaspoon. Confident that he'd been sufficiently distracted, I'd taken out my phone and had dialled Lou's mobile number. *Please answer, Lou.* She'd picked up on the third ring.

"Nicky; where are you?" she'd sounded annoyed, "You're late! The editorial meeting starts in fifteen minutes. Tell me you're outside of the building at the very least."

"Lou," I'd cleared my throat a couple of times, "I'm somewhere near Clapham Junction ..."

"What?" she'd sounded confused, "What do you mean you're *'somewhere near* Clapham Junction'? Don't you know where you are?"

"Not exactly," I'd said, "I'm about twenty minutes' walk away from the station."

"You're about ... *what*?" I'd heard her sharp intake of breath, "Nicky; you sound ... odd. Has something happened?"

"Yeah; you could say that ..."

"*What's* happened? Are you okay?"

"I'm fine Lou ... well, not fine exactly but I'm okay."

"Nicky? You really *do* sound strange. Has something happened with Mike?" she'd asked after a short pause, "Has he done something to ...?"

"No," I'd said quickly, "No; nothing like that ... I promise."

"Then what's wrong?" she'd demanded and I'd been able to hear the first faint tones of panic, "I know something is and ... what the hell are you doing near Clapham Junction?"

"I haven't really got time to explain," I'd bitten my lip, "Lou; I need you to cover my arse ... in more ways than one."

"What do you mean?"

I'd hesitated, "I didn't tell Mike last night that you'd pulled me from Jodie's show. If I had, I wouldn't have been able to catch the early train this morning ... and I needed to be on it. I'm going to switch my phone off for a while once I've ended this call. You know Mike will call you when he can't reach me. Please; tell him you and I had a row this morning; a huge one ..."

# The Runner – Part 1 Nicky's Story

"What? Nicky; you're beginning to scare me. What the hell is going on? Are you sure you're okay? You don't sound at all yourself ..."

"Lou, please. Just tell Mike we had a massive row and as a result you've pulled me from Jodie's slot ... and my own."

"From your own ..." she'd repeated in astonishment, "Why would I tell him that I've pulled you from your own show?"

"I ... I'm not coming in, Lou. Not today ... I'm sorry."

There had been a long pause, "Nicky, are you ill? You really don't sound ... right."

"I'm not ill," I'd promised her, "I'm ... with someone."

"You're ..." she'd gasped in disbelief. Once again there had been a pregnant pause whilst she'd tried to absorb my words and attempt to make sense of them. "Nicky; when you say you're *with* someone," she'd finally ventured, "do you mean you're *with* someone; as in you're playing away from home?"

"Not exactly," I'd answered, "I'm just ... getting to know him." I'd sighed, "I really like him, Lou and ... I want to get to know him better ... *much* better."

"Oh ... my ... God!" I'd been able to hear first her disbelief, then her relief that I really did seem to at least be safe and well, followed by a small chuckle, "Don't tell me that you're finally waking up to smell that coffee ...!"

"I think I might be doing just that ..." I'd sighed, "Please Lou; will you cover my back?"

"Sure," she'd said lightly, "I mean; Oh God! Absolutely! I'll get Steve to cover you ..."

"I meant, will you cover me with Mike?" I'd ventured, "I can't face calling him at the moment. I wouldn't know what to say for one thing."

"Why don't you try something along the lines of *I'm cheating on you ... and so I've taken the day off work; oh and by the way, sense has finally found me so I won't be home either*," she'd chuckled.

"I'm not cheating!" I'd said irritably.

"Yet ...! But you're thinking about it ... aren't you?"

"No! It's not like that! This guy is not like that ... Jesus Lou! *I'm* not like that; you know I'm not."

"Yes, I know ... and it's a pity that you're not!"

I'd sighed, "Lou; will you cover me with Mike or not? I'll ring him a little later but ... I honestly can't face it yet."

"Of course I'll cover you, hun; that goes without saying," she'd said congenially, "But what should I tell him? Just so that you don't drop yourself in it any further when you go home ... you *are* going home, I presume?"

"I'll have to; for now." I'd sighed, "Just tell Mike that you and I had a row and I ... walked out. Yes; tell him that I walked out. He'll enjoy that thought and I might even be able to appease him with it later. He'll assume that I've spent the day 'sulking' as he puts it. Just don't tell him anything more than that."

"Okay ..." she'd said slowly, "I don't have a problem with that. In fact, it will give me great pleasure to know that he'll be chomping at the bit not knowing what's going on."

"Thanks Lou; I really appreciate you doing this for me."

"Hey! Just one minute young Nicholas; don't you dare to hang up on me," I'd heard her tone lighten, "Who is he; this *someone* you're with?"

I'd lowered my voice, "His name's Aaron."

"Aaron?"

"He's the guy from the book store ..."

She'd inhaled a sharp breath, releasing it again as a low whistle, "You're *kidding* me ...?"

"No."

"Good grief; I don't believe it! Well I never ... Good Lord!" she'd sounded as though I had taken the wind from her sails. I probably had. "You know what this is, don't you, Nicky?"

"Madness?" I'd suggested.

"No. It's *Fate*, Nicky;" she'd declared firmly, "That's what it is! Didn't I say so the other day? It's Fate!"

"I don't know about Fate, Lou but it *is* a long story ..." I'd said rather pointedly.

She'd taken the hint. "Yeah, yeah; I get it. You can't tell me now ..."

"Not really."

"But you *will*, Nicky Ashton," she'd said, "Every last gory detail; on Tuesday!"

"I'm not sure that there will be anything *to* tell you."

"If you've got one ounce of sense, sweetheart ... there will be plenty for you to tell me; you'll accept this hand that Fate's dealing you. In fact, I hope to God you will. I've got a good feeling about it ..."

"*You* have?"

She'd laughed, "Yeah, I know; *that*; coming from the most cynical being on the planet. It must tell you something, Nicky."

"It tells me that you must be nuts," I'd said, "As must I be."

"You go for it, sweetheart," she'd said, "Get Mike out of your life once and for all and if it should turn out that this Aaron isn't your Prince Charming ... well, perhaps he's a stepping stone to better things."

"Thanks Lou ..."

"Have fun, sweetie ... and use a condom!"

"Lou! I've told you. It's not like ..."

I'd heard her chuckling over my protest and the line had gone dead before I could finish. *Damn you, Lou!* I'd thought, as my mind had momentarily dared to wonder if Aaron actually *had* any condoms. I knew I hadn't.

I'd been about to switch my phone off when it had beeped, making me jump out of my skin with

## The Runner – Part 1 Nicky's Story

guilt that I hadn't felt I'd yet deserved to own. I'd glanced at the screen to see the text message icon and had taken a deep breath before opening Mike's message. I'd felt myself pale; it seemed I had rung Lou just in time.

*Where the fuck are you? Why isn't your ugly mug staring at me from out of our television set at this very moment? Call me immediately you get this message ... unless you want me to call Lou? And be warned; you'd better have a bloody good explanation ... otherwise you can kiss your precious fucking career goodbye. I'm not kidding, Nicholas ...*

I'd switched my phone off at the same moment as Aaron had returned with two mugs in his hand.

"Hey!" he'd frowned as he'd held one of the mugs out to me, "Are you okay?"

"Thanks," I'd said, accepting the mug gratefully, "Yeah; I'm fine. Why?"

"You look a bit peaky ..."

I'd smiled, "I guess I'm a bit nervous. I've never done anything like this before ..."

He'd raised his eyebrows, "What; you've never had a coffee in a friend's home?"

I'd thought about that for a moment. "No; I don't believe I have," I'd finally said, "Not since I've been with Mike ..." I'd thrown him a small smile, "He really doesn't like me out of his sight; not even for me to go to work ... but that's not what I meant."

"Then what did you mean?"

I'd bitten my lip, "I'd really like to see you again, Aaron ... properly."

"You mean a date?"

I'd nodded, "Yes."

He'd sighed, "And I'd really like to see you, Nicky ... but you're with someone. What is more, you've told me this morning that you're planning to marry him; in little more than three weeks!"

"No, I'm not," I'd shaken my head, "I've never been so frightened in my life, Aaron; not even when I came out but ... the only thing I intend to do is to call it off and tell Mike that I'm leaving him." My eyes had met his, "And before you say anything, it has nothing to do with you. I've been trying to find the courage for almost a year and being with you this morning ... well, I think I might have finally found it."

He hadn't said anything for the longest time. Instead he'd stood rooted to the spot whilst he'd watched me sipping my coffee and I'd fancied that he'd been wrestling with indecision. He'd bitten his lip and had released another heavy sigh.

"When?"

"When will I tell him?" I'd asked, "As soon as I get home."

"No; I meant, when did you want to arrange a date for?"

I'd raised my eyebrows, "I thought you said ..."

"I did," he'd agreed lightly, "But when you're here, in front of me ..."

I'd smiled, "It's a pity you're not free today. I could have taken you for lunch."

He'd hesitated, "I'm off today. I was meeting friends for lunch and then we were going out for the rest of the day ... but I rang and cancelled whilst I was making the coffee."

"So you're free?"

"It would seem so."

"Would you like to come out to lunch with me, Aaron?"

He'd nodded, "Yes please."

"Do you like Italian?"

"*Love* Italian ..." he'd smiled, "My favourite."

"That brings the number to four then ..."

"Four?"

"Four things we have in common," I'd said lightly, "Italian is my favourite food too."

"Do you have a restaurant in mind?" he'd asked.

"Yes, I do actually," I'd smiled at him, "I think we should go back to where this madness began."

He'd laughed and I'd known that he knew the restaurant beneath the arches as well as I did. The word had tumbled from our lips simultaneously.

"Waterloo!"

## **Chapter Thirteen**

"Do you have to get off immediately?" Aaron had asked as he'd closed the front door behind us.

I'd hesitated, already aware of how many hours had elapsed since I'd switched my phone off. Mike was going to be furious enough already but if I'd lingered any longer …

"I really only came back to fetch my laptop, Aaron," I'd said regretfully, "I should be getting back …"

Aaron had nodded his head and bitten his lip, "Course; I understand …"

I'd felt my heart skip a beat to observe the disappointment etched clearly upon his face and I'd thrown him a warm smile, "I do have time for a coffee … if that would be okay?"

"Oh!" His face had brightened and he'd returned my smile, "Yes; good idea. Let me take your coat and then I'll put the kettle on."

I'd removed my coat and had passed it to him, watching as he'd hung it up on the coat hooks behind the front door before shrugging out of his own.

"Come through …" he'd said, leading the way along the hall towards the open door of the kitchen. "It's still only instant, I'm afraid …"

"I like instant," I'd smiled, folding my arms across my chest as I'd leaned against the kitchen counter to watch him fill the kettle.

# The Runner – Part 1 Nicky's Story

He'd plugged the kettle in and had flicked the switch, setting it to boil.

"Thank you, Nicky," he'd said softly, as he'd joined me where I'd stood against the counter, "For lunch."

"Thank you for breakfast," I'd smiled at him, "And for cancelling your plans …"

"I'm glad I did …"

"Me too … although …"

"Although …?" he'd raised his eyebrows quizzically.

"How did you know that I'd even invite you to lunch?"

"I didn't," he'd shaken his head, suddenly looking coy as he'd reached out towards my hands still folded in my arms, "But you were here and … I wasn't anxious for you to leave. I'd hoped to be able to delay you …"

My fingers had sought to entwine gently with his, "How were you planning to delay my leaving …?"

"I haven't the slightest idea …" he'd murmured as he'd tilted his head up towards mine, "I guess I was hoping that if I were to tell you that I didn't have anywhere to go then you wouldn't be in any hurry to leave …"

I'd bent my head slightly until our foreheads were touching, "I'm not in any hurry now," I'd whispered as my arms had slid around his waist.

## The Runner – Part 1 Nicky's Story

"I'm so happy to hear you say so ..." he'd said, wrapping his arms gently around *my* waist and pulling me closer to him.

His lips had brushed lightly against mine and I'd felt his small shiver of anticipation at the same moment that I'd felt my own. I'd closed my eyes; my tongue seeking to part his lips whilst my hand had stolen upwards to lightly trace the route along his back; my thumb gently stroking each nodule of his spine as it passed, before my hand had paused momentarily at the nape of his neck finally becoming entangled in the mop of chestnut hair in a flurry of desperate need and want.

"Oh God ...!" Aaron had murmured, pressing his swollen groin hard against mine when we'd come up for air; the 'click' of the kettle as it finished boiling momentarily breaking the spell. He'd nuzzled his head against my shoulder and my chin had fallen to rest on top of his head, "I want you, Nicky ... so much ..."

I'd swallowed, unable to speak; too afraid of the sudden rush of feelings I'd known I had for him to be able to communicate with words my own desires burning deep within my soul. My hips had begun to gyrate against him almost against my will and one finger had tilted his chin up so that I could find his lips again. His movements had begun to mirror mine ... but to my utter chagrin, I'd frozen when I'd felt his fingers tugging at the buckle of my belt. He'd pulled away instantly to gaze up at me uncertainly.

"Nicky ...?"

"I'm sorry," I'd whispered, "I want to but ..."

### The Runner – Part 1 Nicky's Story

"You're scared," he'd said softly; his hand stroking my cheek. I'd caught it in mine to press it firmly against the side of my face. He'd nodded, "I know you are ... because *he* hurts you."

I'd thrown him a weak smile, "I know what to expect from him ..."

"I would never do anything to hurt you ..."

"I know," I'd whispered; and it had been true. Crazy though it had been, I'd trusted him. I'd shaken my head, "But it still doesn't prevent me from being afraid ..."

He'd contemplated me for a moment or two, his head on one side as though he was trying to choose his words carefully.

"Nicky; do you even *know* what you like ... in bed?"

"What do you mean?"

"I mean there's more to making love than just ... *that*." He'd smiled, "Do you know what you like?"

I'd bitten my lip, "Not really ..."

"Would you like to learn ...?"

"With you ...?"

He'd chuckled, "Well, I wasn't planning on waiting for Kevin ..."

I too had laughed, "Well, good. A threesome is *definitely* not something I'd like; I do know *that* much!"

"It's not my style either," he'd said lightly, "So; something else we have in common!"

"The list grows longer," I'd said, my tone as light as his had been.

"We certainly seem to be quite compatible so far," he'd agreed. He'd sighed, "I'm not going to try and push you into doing anything you don't want to do."

"I know ..."

He'd taken a step away from me, "I'll make the coffee ..."

I'd turned to watch him as he'd taken down two mugs from the cupboard and had pulled open the cutlery drawer; all the while feeling the longing ache in my loins. Perhaps I had been high on the ambience created by the restaurant; perhaps it had been the effects of too much wine; perhaps it had been something far more basic than either of those things. Whatever it was, I'd known that I'd wanted to share all that I had to give with this man; regardless of what it might cost me in the end.

"Aaron ..." He'd turned to face me and had raised his eyebrows, "I don't want coffee ..."

He'd bitten his lip, "You're ready to leave?"

"No," I'd shaken my head and had moved towards him, reaching out to take his hand in mine, "I'm ready to learn ... if you still want to teach me?"

"I'd like us to learn together; what it is that you like ..." he'd whispered, pulling me into the circle of his embrace once more and crushing his lips to mine, "But if you want to stop at any time ..."

"Take me to bed ..." I'd murmured into his ear.

He'd gently kissed my lips once more before he'd released me to take me by the hand and guide me with unhurried steps along the hall and up the stairs; the slow, measured pace serving only to increase the anticipation. Outside of a closed door at the furthest end of the landing, Aaron had paused; the question burning in his eyes. I'd nodded and had taken a deep breath as he'd pushed open the door to his bedroom, my heart beginning to race as my eyes had been drawn to the neatly made double bed in the centre of the room.

"We'll take our time ..." he'd murmured as he'd pulled me into his arms once more and when his hands had finally found my belt again, I hadn't hesitated; I'd been distracted with a belt of my own.

**oOo**

I'd felt neither guilt nor shame when I'd woken up in Aaron's bed at half past three in the afternoon. The caged bird that was my soul had finally been set free and as it had spread its wings, I'd been blissfully happy, perfectly serene and more content than I had ever been able to recall feeling at any other time in my life. I'd smiled to myself when Aaron's arms had tightened around me as he'd felt me stir.

"Hey!" he'd whispered before kissing the top of my head.

"Hey!" I'd whispered back, tilting my head just far enough to kiss the stubble beneath his chin.

"You okay?" he'd asked.

# The Runner – Part 1 Nicky's Story

"Yeah; are you?"

"A bit shell-shocked I think," he'd answered. "Just to clear something up; I *never* do this; not on a first date."

My heart had sunk, "Are you regretting it already?"

I'd thought he had heard my disappointment for he'd slid out from beneath where I'd lain draped halfway across his chest and had turned onto his side to face me whilst his hand had reached out to stroke my cheek.

"God, no!" he'd said, "No; I have *no* regrets, Nicky and I don't want you to think that I do. I'm telling you because I'd hate you to think that I'm an easy lay. I'm not and I never have been." He'd chuckled, "In fact I take a good deal of wining and dining as a rule; so much so that most guys don't hang around for long."

I'd finally allowed myself to smile, "You don't sleep around then?"

"No," he'd looked amused, "Which is why I have a pretty good grip ..."

"Yeah, I'd noticed that," I'd said lightly before I'd sighed. "Aaron; you need to know that I don't do this either. Not ever. I've had two sexual partners in my life ... and one of them was my ex-wife; just to clear that up."

He'd nodded, "And you're engaged to the other ..."

At his reference to Mike, I'd rolled over onto my back and covered my eyes with my arm whilst my stomach had lurched with the fear of what I had to do once I returned home. "Yes," I'd agreed, turning my head on the pillow to look at him, "But I've already told you; I won't be; not for much longer."

He'd nodded his head slowly and had bitten his lip, "Perhaps I'm selfish; I don't know … but I rather hope that you mean that …"

"I do …"

"… because I really want to see you again, Nicky …"

"And I want to see you …" I'd interrupted quickly.

"I'm glad that you do," he'd said quietly, "but you need to know that I won't be your 'bit on the side'. Whether this … *we* … could go anywhere or not, it would have to be all or nothing for me. I couldn't settle for anything less."

"And *I* couldn't give you anything less …" I'd shaken my head, "Is this real? I mean … it feels like some totally absurd dream from which I'm going to wake up at any moment. Not that I'd want to change any of it …"

He'd smiled, "It's been a totally surreal day I grant you but I wouldn't change one moment of it either; especially *these* moments; making love with you and being able to hold you in my arms. I never want to let you go."

"And I don't want you to …"

He'd smiled, "It really is beginning to feel like Destiny …"

"Yes, it is," I'd agreed with a heavy sigh, "But whether it is or it isn't, I'll have to go soon."

"You don't have to go ..."

"Yes I do. I don't want to but I have to. I'm dreading it but ..." I'd sighed again, "I know it's cowardly but God it would be so much easier if he wasn't there; if he was still working. If I could just have all of my bags packed and the taxi already booked before he got home from work; you know?"

"Where will you go?"

"To Lou's ..." I'd told him, "She's already said that I can move in with her; just until I get back on my feet."

"Or you could stay here ..." he'd ventured tentatively.

I'd raised my eyebrows, "Here?"

"Why not?"

"Why ...?" I'd laughed, "Aaron; we've only just met!"

"I know ... and you're already in my bed."

I'd shaken my head, "It's hardly the same thing as moving in with you ... tempting though it is. Besides; wouldn't your housemates have something to say about it? Never mind your landlord!"

"Kevin wouldn't have a problem with it and I don't see that my other two housemates would have a problem with it ... and I'm quite sure my landlord wouldn't. He's a really nice guy ... though he'll probably still double the rent!"

I'd laughed, "It's an absurd notion ..."

## The Runner – Part 1 Nicky's Story

"This whole thing is absurd ..."

"That's true ..." I'd agreed.

"Then stay ..."

"Aaron; I can't ..."

"Why?"

"You know why," I'd said, releasing another heavy sigh, "I have to go home. I have to face *him* ... even though it'll be the hardest thing I've ever had to do. Not because I still have feelings for him," I'd hastened to add, "but because it's the right thing to do. Besides, I need to collect some clothes at the very least."

"We can buy you some clothes; tomorrow. Until then you can use anything of mine. It's only your trousers you will have to wear again tomorrow since mine on you would look as though they were divorcing your ankles to marry your knees ... unless you want to borrow a pair of shorts ..." he'd looked amused.

"You make it all sound so simple ..."

"It is; stay. We'll go shopping in the morning and then spend the rest of the weekend in bed. What could be simpler than that?"

"Aaron ... please don't," I'd shaken my head, "You have no idea of how close I am to giving in to temptation ... but I can't stay. I have to go; I have to tell him face-to-face. After three years, I owe him that much ... regardless that I no longer love him."

He'd bitten his lip and had shaken his head, "If you go ... I don't think you'll come back."

# The Runner – Part 1 Nicky's Story

"I will," I'd said firmly. "Aaron; I won't lie to you. I'm shitting myself at the thought of going back and I know that it's going to take every ounce of my strength and resolve to walk out of that front door but I will ..." I'd smiled at him, "*You've* given me the courage to do it and when all is said and done, what can Mike possibly do to stop me? His true power lies in the fact that I'm under his roof. I see that now."

"From all that you've told me of him, Nicky, he'll find a way," he'd said glumly, "I know his type. He'll have some trick up his sleeve; you mark my words."

"And whatever it is, I'll be ready for it." I'd said softly. "Aaron; I've known you for all of five minutes so for me to tell you now that I love you would seem downright foolish and infantile ... and I won't say the words until I know beyond all doubt that I really mean them." I'd sighed and my fingers had stolen to interlock with his, "I can't explain any of *this* but whatever it is, it feels very *real* ... and I think it's far more powerful than either of us." I'd smiled at him and had reached up to kiss his lips, "I won't be able to *help* coming back, Aaron because in finding you, it feels like I've finally come home."

He'd sighed, seemingly resigned to accepting my decision. His hand had gently run across my chest and his mouth had reached up to cover mine.

"Then I think I should remind you where home is; at least one last time before you go ..." he'd murmured, "Just in case you get lost on your way back."

## The Runner – Part 1 Nicky's Story

"I won't get lost but God, yes; please remind me ... imprint it upon my heart; just in case ..."

**oOo**

I'd watched Aaron walking away from the station, the warmth of his kiss still lingering on my lips; his scent filling my nostrils and when I'd momentarily closed my eyes I had still been able to feel his arms wrapped around me in a tight embrace; hear the soft lisp in my ear as he'd made his last plea.

"Pack your bags and come straight back," he'd whispered just before he'd loosened his grip, "Please Nicky ..."

"Aaron; we've been through this ..." I'd sighed, "I promised I would come back first thing in the morning and stay until Sunday night ..."

"If you stay with him for even one more night ..." he'd shaken his head, "You've said yourself that he's not stupid; that he'll probably be expecting something like this after your silence all day." He'd sighed, "He's had all day to plan his attack ..."

With Aaron's words still ringing in my ears, I'd entered the station, switching my phone on whilst I'd walked. Almost immediately I'd been alerted to the fact that I'd received no texts but had a voicemail message. I hadn't needed to be Einstein to know that the single voicemail would be from Mike. My heart thumping madly in my chest, I'd dialled into my voicemail service to listen to Mike's message. His soft, almost contrite tone had surprised me more than the lack of text messages.

*"Hi Angel; it's only me. I'm sorry for the hateful text message I sent you this morning. I know you've turned your phone off and I can't say that I blame you. I've cancelled the weekend trip ..."*

Shit! I'd been so caught up inside of Aaron's sphere that I had completely forgotten that I should have already been making my way towards Mike in the hotel. I'd listened to the remainder of his voicemail message; his soothing tones doing nothing to stem the rising tide of fear.

*"... Just come home, Nicky. I know that you're scared; but everything's going to be alright; you'll see. I really am sorry about that text. If I could take it back, I would. I've spoken to Lou and she told me what happened between you both this morning. I'm sorry, Nicky. I jumped to the wrong conclusion. Please come home, baby ... and give me a chance to explain."*

I'd dialled his mobile number as I'd descended the steps to the platform; half wishing that I'd left Aaron earlier to catch a less crowded service and part of me wishing that I'd had the guts to stay. No matter how ridiculous it had sounded even to me, some sixth sense had been convinced that it was in Aaron's arms that I had been meant to wake up; tomorrow and every day that followed. *Ridiculous; get a grip, Nicky Ashton! He'll turn out to be nothing more than a foolish one-night stand ... or rather; a one afternoon-stand!* One night-stand; Christ! I couldn't even get *that* right.

## The Runner – Part 1 Nicky's Story

"Nicky? Oh thank God! I've been worried sick ..." Mike's relief had been audible; not that I'd felt an ounce of guilt.

"Hey!" I'd said sheepishly.

"Where are you?"

"Clapham Junction ..."

"So you're on your way home?"

"Yes ..."

"Are you alright?"

"I'm fine ..."

"Where have you been all day?"

I'd taken a deep breath, "Just wandering around," I'd lied, grateful that he hadn't been beside me to see the lie burning in my cheeks.

"Wandering around; where?"

"Here and there; thinking; you know?"

"Thinking; about us?"

I'd bitten my lip as though doing so would somehow give me the courage I'd need. Even just the sound of his voice had been enough to make me feel uneasy; and he hadn't even been ranting. "Amongst other things ..."

"What things?"

"Well; my career ..."

I'd heard him sigh, "Nicky; we'll talk once you get home but ... you know this is just another of your panic attacks; right?" He'd filled the gap when I'd failed to respond. "Look; I know I surprised you the other night ... though God knows why I should have after three years together ..."

"You did," I'd said; the first honest thing I'd said in a long while.

"With the proposal ... or with the notion of getting married in three weeks?"

"Both ..." I'd said quietly. "I was still trying to process the ring on my finger, Mike ..."

He'd sighed again, "We'll talk ... and then you'll understand; but really, Nicky; there's no need for you to be scared. Everything will be as it has been until now." *I don't doubt that it will; and that's why I'm so scared!* "The only difference being that we will be married. Okay?"

It hadn't been *okay* but I'd heard myself dutifully agreeing that it was. He'd sounded satisfied when he'd spoken again.

"I'll pick you up from the station."

"I can walk ..."

"I know you can ... but I'll be waiting for you just the same."

*Yeah; I bet you will. And this time I'll be ready for you.*

## Chapter Fourteen

"Nicky?"

I'd looked up to meet Mike's eyes across the dining table and I'd swallowed, wondering if he'd once again been counting the number of times I'd pushed food into my mouth. A quick glance down at my plate had been enough to reassure me that I'd succeeded in forcing down most of the meal he'd prepared. I'd watched him set down his own cutlery on his plate, positioning it in the accepted manner to indicate that he'd finished. He'd raised his eyebrows at me enquiringly and I'd known that the moment I'd been dreading had finally arrived.

"Mike ..." I'd begun, wriggling in my seat and reaching for the glass of wine he'd poured me at the start of the meal but which I hadn't yet touched. His manner had been perfectly serene thus far but the glass of red before me had been enough for me to be in no doubt that Mike was pissed at me; regardless of any words which had left his mouth to contradict him. One glass of red wine set before me had been all it had taken to drain me of the courage Aaron had left me with at Clapham Junction.

I'd felt sick as I'd recalled Aaron's assertion that Mike had an Ace up his sleeve. In truth, I'd already known for myself that he would have but safe in Aaron's arms I'd thought I was ready to take Mike on. I wasn't. I'd known that now. I should have stayed in London with Aaron; should have listened to him. I'd bitten down hard on my lip as I'd fought back the tears. I could have been in Aaron's arms now; feeling the silken touch of his lips brushing mine; inhaling the sweet scent of his

## The Runner – Part 1 Nicky's Story

cologne; feeling the warmth of his body pressed hard against mine as we made love. It had all been there for the taking ... and I'd rejected all that he'd been offering me. Regret, it seemed, was to be my companion for tonight.

I'd struggled to give Mike my attention whilst he'd waited, scrutinising me carefully. I'd cleared my throat, tossed back almost half of the foul red liquid and had tried to sit up straighter in my seat.

"Mike," I'd tried again, "I'm really sorry ..."

He'd raised his eyebrows, "For ...?"

"I didn't mean to ruin the weekend ..."

"Oh. I thought you meant that you were sorry for going AWOL on me without a word ..."

"I'm sorry for that too ..."

"Why didn't you call me?"

"What?" I'd stared at him, "Mike; you sent me such a hateful text message. Would *you* have called you if you had been me?"

"Yes; I rather think that I would," he'd said serenely, "If not just to put me out of my misery and stop me from worrying about you, Nicky. But then I'm not the selfish, spoiled brat that you are; so perhaps I shouldn't have expected anything else from you."

"Selfish?" My eyes had widened, "I'm not selfish ..."

"Yes you are ..."

"I'm not! I was *afraid,* Mike!"

"Afraid? Of what?"

I'd bitten my lip, the single word reaching him across the table as little more than a whisper, "You."

"Me?" he'd raised his eyebrows, "Oh, I get it. One text message ... a little inappropriate perhaps, I grant you ..."

"*A little inappropriate?*" I'd gasped in disbelief. Had I dreamt his voicemail apology of earlier? No; of course I hadn't. It had been Mike being Mike. I'd shocked him by my silence today and the message had merely been intended to lull me into a false sense of security; carefully constructed to lure me home and I'd known in that moment that he hadn't believed Lou any more than he'd believed me now.

"... but one text message and suddenly your selfishness and lack of consideration becomes *my* fault!" he'd continued as if I hadn't spoken.

"If you *hadn't* sent it, I *would* have called you!" I'd said defensively, almost believing my own lie, "In fact, I'd been about to ... and then I got that text ..." I'd stared at my plate, "I hate it when you do that ... and you do it often."

"Oh what a bloody Drama Queen ..."

"That's not fair, Mike," I'd shaken my head, still unable to look at him, "I hate your temper ... and it's been getting worse of late. Such messages don't bode well; not for me. You scare me when you're in those moods ... and you scared me again today. I didn't want to come home. I was afraid to."

"Bullshit!" he'd retorted, "All you had to do was to call and tell me that you and Lou had fought."

# The Runner – Part 1 Nicky's Story

*Yeah; and the minute I'd called, I'd have had no choice but to come home. I didn't want to.*

I'd sighed, "I'm sorry; my head was all over the place. I should have called you."

"You should damned well have come home the minute you'd left the studios!" he'd snapped; his tone forcing me to look up at him. I'd watched him draining the last of his wine, when without warning his wine glass had suddenly come hurtling across the table towards me. I'd jumped to my feet, pushing my chair back, hearing it scrape against the floor as I'd tried to remove myself from harm's way. I'd turned my head towards the glass at the very moment it shattered onto the hardwood floor, shards of glass flying in every direction. "Where the *fuck* have you been all day, Nicky; huh? Tell me; I demand to know; now!"

"I've already told you; walking …"

"Walking; *all fucking day*?"

"Yes …"

"Where?"

"I … I don't know; I can't remember!"

"You can't remember? Pah! A likely story …"

"It's not; I really can't remember …" I'd said desperately, backing away as he'd risen to his feet, "I remember walking along Embankment at some point …" I'd said quickly, already holding my palms out towards him; a defensive stance.

"Liar!" he'd reached me in three strides and had caught me firmly by my upper arm, his other hand striking me across the face so hard that the burn in my cheek had been instant. "Again; where have you been?"

"I've already told you …"

Another strike across my face and this time I had tasted blood. Whether his strike had split my lip or my own teeth had been the cause, I hadn't known. I'd begun to tremble as he'd held both of my arms securely in his grip, shaking me sufficiently to make my teeth rattle in their gums. His face had been puce and contorted in fury as he'd pushed it into mine.

"Last chance; tell me where you've been … and think carefully before you answer, Nicholas …"

I'd shaken my head, unable to speak. *Fight back, Nicky; you're a grown man, for God's sake; fight back!* I hadn't been able to, frozen as I was by fear.

"Who is he, Nicky?"

"W … what?"

"The man you've been with; who is he?"

"I haven't …"

"LIAR!"

He'd released one of my arms and had drawn back his free arm to strike me with such force that he'd sent me hurtling across the room towards the lounge where I'd fallen to the floor, narrowly missing striking my head against the solid oak arm of the sofa. He'd moved to stand over me, where shock had left me nailed to the floor, rendering me incapable of doing anything other than to look up at him helplessly whilst I'd rubbed at the raw sting in my cheek.

"*Who ... is ... he?*"

"There is no 'he' ..."

"LIAR!" he'd drawn his leg back and had kicked me in the thigh with all the strength he could muster.

A scream had escaped my throat as I'd felt the pain and I'd slid back until I'd been resting against the side of the sofa. His steps had followed me. "Mike! Please ..."

"I can *smell* him on you, Nicholas. You *reek* of him ... the *car* reeks of him!"

"No ..." I'd shaken my head furiously in denial as the tears had finally spilled, "You're wrong; you've got it wrong ..."

"No, I haven't!" he'd reached towards me and had hauled me up to my feet by my hair before grabbing my arm again and forcing it up painfully behind my back whilst he'd pushed his face into mine. "I'll ask you once more; who is he?"

"There isn't anyone ..."

"Liar!" With my arm still twisted behind my back, he'd spun me around and pulled me against him so that my back was pressed securely against his chest. His other arm had risen to press tightly around my throat, "You were seen, Nicky!" he'd hissed into my ear.

"W ... what?"

"Yes, that's right, *sweetheart*. You didn't know that Errol was in town today, did you? He had an appointment with his specialist at St. Thomas's; he saw you and some bloke entering Waterloo station together just after one o'clock. So; care to tell me who this bloke was?"

"Mike ..." my free hand had tried to pull his arm away from my throat, "I ... I can't ... breathe ..."

"Then tell me what I want to know and I'll let you go ..."

"He ... he's a friend; that's all," I'd spluttered, "I spent the afternoon with an old friend ..."

"An old friend?"

"Yes ... we were friends at college. I haven't seen him for a few years ... I bumped into him today; we had lunch ..."

"Then why lie about it ... if he's just an old friend?"

"I ... I don't know ..."

"You don't know?"

"No ..."

"Did you lie because you slept with him, perhaps?"

"What? No! Of course I didn't ..."

"Is that so? Then why do you reek of him?"

"I don't know; I was upset ..." I'd choked out as the tears had streamed freely down my cheeks; the excretions from my nose running down to coat my lips, "He hugged me ... that's it, Mike; I swear ... that's it. I guess his after-shave is strong; I don't know ... but it's not what you think. I swear he's just an old friend from college ... and he's straight!"

# The Runner – Part 1 Nicky's Story

"You were hugged by a *straight* man?"

"Men *do* hug men without it meaning anything, Mike ..."

His grip around my throat and around my arm twisted up behind my back had relaxed a little. "What's his name?"

"John ..."

"John what?"

"I ... I don't remember."

"Liar!"

"I'm not; I don't think I *ever* knew his surname! I've told you; I haven't seen him for a few years. I bumped into him; he invited me for lunch at his house ..."

"Where does he live?"

"Vauxhall ..."

He'd pulled my head back into his shoulder by my hair, "If I find out that you're lying to me, Nicky ..."

"I'm not ..."

Finally, he'd released me, pushing me away as he did so and causing me to stumble. Without looking at me, he'd moved past me and had thrown himself onto the sofa.

"Go and take a shower," he'd said, picking up the television remote, "You smell like some cheap trick ..." I'd heard him chuckle, "I'd tell you to tell your friend, John to invest in a decent cologne ... except you won't be seeing him again to pass on the message. Do I make myself clear?"

## The Runner – Part 1 Nicky's Story

"Yes," I'd answered in a small voice.

He'd placed one hand behind his ear, "Didn't hear you …"

"Yes!"

"Good. Now, go and shower … and do a thorough job whilst you're in the bathroom; I'm sure you get my drift."

## Chapter Fifteen

I'd barely locked the bathroom door behind me when I'd felt my stomach beginning to heave. The sink had been closer than the toilet bowl and I'd vomited until I'd been sure that even the lining of my stomach had left along with the meal that only a short while ago had been on my plate. My legs trembling and shock setting in, I'd stumbled to the closed lid of the toilet and had sat down. My body had shaken violently from head to toe whilst I'd sobbed silently into my cupped hands. If Aaron hadn't thought I'd cut a pathetic figure this morning, I'd been sure that he'd soon change his mind had he been able to see me now.

Almost as soon as I'd thought of Aaron, I'd felt my phone vibrate in the pocket of my trousers and I'd pulled it out to see the envelope icon displayed in the middle of the screen. I'd opened it and had felt my heart breaking as I'd read his words.

*Hey babe! Missing you already; so much that it hurts. I've told Kevin that you were here today. He knows all about you of course. He couldn't believe it and can't decide if I'm a lucky bastard or just plain nuts! I know I'm not nuts. Not now. It all feels so ... right; you know? Although I have to admit that even I'm wondering if it was just some beautiful dream! Please tell me it wasn't. I know what you said about love and saying the words but ... I think I might be falling in love with you, Nicky; I have been for these past three months ... and I had to tell you. If I didn't I would never be able to sleep tonight; if I even do. I'm not sure that I will as I can't stop thinking about you*

## The Runner – Part 1 Nicky's Story

*and wishing that you were here in my arms. See you tomorrow; can't wait. A. xx*

I'd read Aaron's text message through three times, feeling calmer each time I had. By the time I'd begun to type out my reply, my courage had begun to surface again. I could do this. All I had to do was tell Mike that I'd had enough – especially after tonight – pack my bags and leave. How hard could that be; not least when my destiny – which I had been certain Aaron was – would be waiting for me with open arms and a heart filled with love at the other end.

*Hey sweetie! If it was a dream then we've both shared in it ... and I'm glad for it. Missing you too and my heart is already aching to be with you; and I will be; in the morning; bags packed as promised. Hope you're prepared for the fact that I might not leave after all ... N. xx*

His reply had come back almost instantly. *I'll sleep on your side of the bed tonight; to keep it warm for you. A. xx*

I'd smiled to myself. *I have a side of the bed ...?*

*Of course ... the side right next to me.*

I'd bitten my lip before texting my final reply. *Don't text again tonight. It's difficult here but it's going to be okay. I think I could fall in love with you too. Just had to say it ... and no; I'm not nuts either; scared but not nuts. I'll be thinking of you every moment until I'm in your arms again and you are in mine. N. xx*

I'd almost jumped out of my skin when I'd heard Mike tapping on the bathroom door. His

# The Runner – Part 1 Nicky's Story

gentle tone had been more than a little disconcerting and had it not been for my swollen lip, the pain in my thigh, the bruise I could already feel beginning to emerge on my cheek and the ache in my arm and shoulder where my arm had been pinned up behind my back, I might have begun to wonder if I'd imagined the whole after dinner scene between Mike and me.

"Are you going to be long, Angel?" he'd purred softly through the door, "Should I put the coffee on yet?"

"I ... no; I mean; don't wait for me. I don't think I want any coffee thanks ..."

"Nicky? Are you alright, sweetheart? You don't sound too good."

"I'm ... not feeling very well. I haven't had my shower yet ..."

"What's wrong?"

*What's wrong? You've just knocked the shit out of me; scared me out of my wits. What the hell could possibly be wrong?*

"Nothing; I've been a bit sick ... that's all."

"Sick? Do you think you're coming down with something? I mean, it can't have been dinner because I'm alright."

"It wasn't dinner ..."

"Nicky; open the door. You really don't sound very well ..."

"I'll be alright. You go and make your coffee ..."

"Open the door ..."

## The Runner – Part 1 Nicky's Story

"I'm fine; really ..."

"Nicky; please don't make me break the door down ..."

I'd taken a deep breath and had risen from where I'd been sitting on the lid of the toilet seat, taking care to conceal my phone deep within my pocket once more, praying that Aaron would pay heed to my last text, for if he didn't, although the device was set to silent, Mike would be sure to hear it vibrate. I'd crossed the bathroom, unlocked the door and had pulled it open.

Mike had smiled at me, his brow creasing into a sudden frown as he'd raised his hand to lightly stroke my still burning cheek.

"Jesus, Nicky! What have you done?" he'd gasped, looking past me into the bathroom as though he'd expected to be greeted by chaos, "Have you fallen?"

"What?"

"Your cheek; you've got a hell of a bruise forming ... and what the hell have you done to your lip? It's bleeding ..."

I'd stared at him, wiping my hand across my lip, unable to speak. Was he serious?

His frown had deepened, "What?"

I'd shaken my head, "Nothing."

"How have you done that?" he'd asked, striding to the sink and turning on the cold tap before grabbing a flannel and holding it beneath the flow of the water. I'd watched him wring the piece of towelling cloth out and refold it into a perfect square. "Come here and sit down," he'd said, indicating the toilet seat. He'd pressed the flannel gingerly against my cheek and had winced when I had. "That looks sore, Angel," he'd said softly, "What the hell happened? Did you slip; or did you open the bathroom cabinet too quickly?"

"Are you kidding me, Mike?"

"What do you mean?"

I'd stared at him open mouthed before I'd shaken my head again, "It doesn't matter." I'd bitten my lip, "I don't remember what happened ..."

"You said you'd been sick; did you pass out?"

"I don't know; maybe ..."

His eyes had flicked around the bathroom fittings and when he'd spoken again, I'd realised he'd been making a show of looking for blood.

"Well, you might have cut you lip but luckily your head appears to be intact ..." he'd run his hand gently over my scalp, "Nope; no lumps or bumps," he'd smiled at me, "It would seem that your cheek has taken the brunt of it, sweetheart. You must have fallen against the sink or the toilet when you passed out."

"Yeah; I guess I must have ..."

"I wonder what brought that on. It seems to have happened very suddenly."

"I wonder ..."

He'd smiled, "You know; I don't think I like the idea of you getting in the shower; not if you're unwell. If you should slip or fall or pass out again ..." he'd shuddered, "It doesn't bear thinking about."

## The Runner – Part 1 Nicky's Story

"I'm sure I'll be fine now …"

"Even so," he'd held out his hand to pull me to my feet, frowning again when I'd sucked in a breath.

"What's the matter?"

"My arm; well, my shoulder …"

"You've hurt your arm too?"

"It would seem so."

"Right; that decides it. No shower tonight; not for you. I think it would be better if you were to just climb into bed."

I'd nodded, "Perhaps an early night would be a good idea, although …"

"Although what, Nicky?"

"Mike; we still need to talk; about what happened today … well, about everything that's happened this week."

"Yes, I know," he'd sighed, "I know you have things that you want to say to me … and there are things that I need to say to you too. I should have told you long ago but …" he'd shaken his head and had smiled. "Do you think you're able to stand up now?"

I'd nodded, "I'm fine; really."

"Well, nonetheless; let me help you," he'd wrapped his arm around my waist and had guided me out of the bathroom and back into the lounge where he'd helped me onto the sofa. "That's it, Angel; gently does it." He'd swung my legs up onto the sofa, "Just rest. I know you don't want coffee;

not if you've been sick but how about a nice cup of sweet, black tea? It usually does the trick for you ..."

"Thanks ... that'd be nice," I'd smiled up at him, as I'd fought to hide from him my growing unease.

"Hey! Don't look so worried," he'd leaned towards me and had kissed my forehead, "I'm not angry with you, Nicky; okay? I know that you think things have moved a little too quickly ... but I have my reasons. You'll understand soon enough and really; why should you be so scared? We've had three wonderful years together ..." He'd smiled a little sadly, "Please don't look at me like that ..."

"Like what?"

"As though you fear me ..."

"I'm not ..."

He'd shaken his head, "You are and for the life of me I don't know why you should. Have I ever given you a reason to be afraid of me?"

*Many.* I'd shaken my head, "No ..."

"I don't know; you and your panic attacks. Perhaps we should talk to the doctor about them ..."

"I'm not having a panic attack."

"I think you are, sweetheart ... and they seem to be getting out of control. Why else would you have been so sick and passed out tonight?"

"I can't think ..."

# The Runner – Part 1 Nicky's Story

He'd leaned towards me to kiss my forehead, "Just rest; I won't be long ... and then we'll talk ..." He'd shaken his head as he'd looked down at me and his hand had once again reached out to caress my bruised cheek, "Silly boy ... I really can't afford to let you out of my sight ..." he'd murmured, his words sending a shiver of fear up my spine before he'd left me to my thoughts.

**oOo**

I hadn't heard him return and I'd been startled to hear his voice.

"Sweetheart," he'd said softly, holding a mug out towards me, "I've made it nice and sweet. Drink it whilst it's hot."

"Thanks ..."

"How are you feeling?"

"Okay ..."

He'd nodded, "Can I sit down?"

I'd slid my legs over to make room for him to perch on the sofa beside me, wincing at the pain which had shot through my thigh.

"What's wrong?"

"My leg hurts ..."

He'd raised his eyebrows, "Your leg? What have you done?"

I'd closed my eyes, "Don't know ..."

"Let me see ..."

# The Runner – Part 1 Nicky's Story

"It's nothing ..."

"Let me see ..."

Moments later we were both examining the swollen bruise which had already grown to be almost the size of a saucer.

"Jesus, Nicky? How did you do that?"

I'd hesitated, "Must have happened when I fell ..."

He'd shaken his head, "I'm going to call Les tomorrow. Friend or no friend, he'll charge me an arm and a leg for a weekend callout but still ..." he'd leaned towards me to plant a kiss on my lips, "What's that compared to your health, huh?"

"I don't need a doctor; there's nothing wrong with me."

"I think we'll leave that to Les to decide, Angel," he'd said firmly, "These panic attacks are out of control. Perhaps some tranquilisers will help ..."

"No!" I'd protested, horrified, "I'm fine. I don't have panic attacks ... I fell; that's all; tired probably ..."

"Shush ... just rest. Don't upset yourself ..." he'd sighed, "Although perhaps that's going to be unavoidable ..."

"What do you mean?"

"Nicky; there's something I need to tell you; something I should have told you long ago," he'd reached for my hand to take it in his, "Sweetheart; there's a reason why I don't want to wait to get married."

## The Runner – Part 1 Nicky's Story

His cadence had been off, forcing me to look at him more closely, "Oh?"

"I've not been very well, Nicky; not very well at all, in fact."

I'd swallowed as I'd felt the heavy weight pressing against my heart, "What's wrong?"

"I've managed to hide it from you for quite a while now …" he'd smiled weakly at me, "But this afternoon, when I'd read back that horrible text message I'd sent you, I realised that I was going to have to tell you; so that you could understand what's happening to me. I don't remember writing it to be perfectly honest with you, never mind sending it … but I often don't remember the things that I do these days."

"Mike …"? I'd ventured nervously, "You're scaring me …"

"I know … and I'm sorry. I don't want you to be scared, Nicky but you do need to be prepared."

"Prepared …?"

He'd nodded, "I've been having some terrible headaches for quite some time now …"

"You've never said …"

"No; I know," he'd replied, "I didn't want to worry you … but I'm afraid that time is long since passed." His eyes had been full of sorrow as they'd met mine, "I have a large tumour, Nicky; on my brain."

My eyes had widened in shock and horror, "A tumour?" I'd repeated weakly, "What sort of tumour?"

# The Runner – Part 1 Nicky's Story

"The kind that's malignant ..." he'd said simply, making me gasp. "I'm sorry my Angel but there's no easy way to say this. It's gone far too far for chemo and it's inoperable ..." He'd reached out to stroke my cheek, "I know you haven't found some of my ... moods ... easy to take of late but now you know why. I haven't been able to help it; it's the tumour pressing against my brain."

"No!" I'd shaken my head in denial, "No! There must be something they can do ..."

"There isn't," he'd said, "I've seen the best doctors in the country and there's nothing that can be done now. The cancer has advanced too far ... I'm dying, Nicky. They've given me three to six months ..."

"Oh my God!" I'd burst into tears, spilling my tea all over me but barely able to feel the scalding liquid; numb as I was in my shock. I'd felt Mike take the mug from my hands and moments later I had been in his arms whilst he'd rocked me.

"That's it baby; have a good cry," he'd murmured whilst he'd gently stroked my hair, "I'm so sorry. I didn't want to tell you ... I wasn't *going* to tell you." I'd heard him sigh, "But then I realised that you had a right to know; you had a right to know *before* I proposed to you."

"Oh, Mike ..." I'd sobbed into his shoulder.

"It's going to be alright, sweetheart; *you're* going to be alright," he'd murmured soothingly, "We don't need to get married if you don't want to ... and really; why should you want to marry a dying man? You're still so young; too young to be a widower. Marrying you would have made me the happiest

## The Runner – Part 1 Nicky's Story

man alive but I was being selfish; to you. I see that now. I've left you well provided for in my Will so you won't have to worry ..."

"Mike; don't ..." I'd shaken my head, "I don't want to hear it."

He'd chuckled softly beside my ear, "You have to hear it, Nicky. Marriage would have made me happy and protected you ... from my family. They may hate me but they don't hate my money. They'll fight you of course and without our sealing our Civil Partnership, you'll be weaker against them ..."

"I don't care! I don't want your money; I never wanted your money!"

"No; I know ... but the thing is, Nicky, I don't want those bastards to have it. I want every last penny to go to you ... and Finn and Molly; set the kids up for life ..." He'd straightened up, reaching out to wipe away my tears with his thumb, smiling at me all the while, "Anyway; it hardly matters now. You don't want to marry a dying man ... perhaps you shouldn't ..."

"Mike ..."

"Well, you don't; do you?"

I'd swallowed as the guilt had washed over me whilst I'd tried to push away the sickening thoughts racing through my mind.

*No, I don't want to marry you. I feel awful for you; I really do ... but I don't love you. I want to see what I might have with Aaron ... I know there's something there between us; something real and honest and good; I can feel it; taste it ...*

# The Runner – Part 1 Nicky's Story

*Shame on you, Nicky Ashton! Three to six months' more of your life; is it really too much to give to a dying man who once loved you; who you once loved in return? Besides; he's had a tumour growing in his brain; perhaps he really hasn't been able to help himself and perhaps he really doesn't remember the awful things he says and does to you; after all, it wasn't always like this, was it?*

"Nicky; sweetheart?"

"Hmmm?"

"*Do* you still want to get married?"

"I don't want your money; any of it ..."

He'd laughed, "What you do with it once I'm gone is up to you. I hope you'll change your mind of course but still ..." His face had grown serious again, "Forget the money. Do you love me enough that you could still marry me; even though I'm going to have to leave you soon?"

The tears had washed my cheeks afresh whilst I'd slowly nodded my head, "Yes ..." I'd whispered, "Of course I do."

"Oh God, Nicky!" he'd pulled me into his tight embrace again, "I love you so much ..."

"I love you too ..."

"So; in three weeks' time ...?" he'd whispered into my ear.

"Yes ..."

"And what about your job?" he'd murmured, "I don't want to waste a moment with you ..."

"I'll resign ..." I'd promised.

"Just you and me ... until the end?"

"Just you and me, Mike ... until the end; I promise."

"Thank you, Nicky. I mean it; you've made me so happy ..." he'd sat up and had smiled, "Let me make you another tea ... I think you could probably do with the sugar; it's good for shock."

As soon as I'd been alone, I'd reached into my pocket to withdraw my mobile phone. With the tears streaming down my face, I'd tapped out just three words.

*I'm so sorry.*

After the briefest hesitation, I'd pressed 'send' and had deleted all of my text messages and with them Aaron's number.

*Goodbye Aaron ...*

Printed in Great Britain
by Amazon.co.uk, Ltd.,
Marston Gate.